witch baby and me

at school

Debi Gliori

WITCH BABY AND ME AT SCHOOL
A CORGI BOOK 978 0 552 55677 4

Published in Great Britain by Corgi Books,
an imprint of Random House Children's Books
A Random House Group Company

This edition published 2009

1 3 5 7 9 10 8 6 4 2

The Random House Group Limited supports the Forest Stewardship Council
(FSC), the leading international forest certification organization.
All our titles that are printed on Greenpeace-approved FSC-certified
paper carry the FSC logo. Our paper procurement policy can be
found at www.rbooks.co.uk/environment.

Set in Adobe Garamond Pro 14/14pt

Corgi Books are published by Random House Children's Books,
61–63 Uxbridge Road, London W5 5SA

www.**kids**at**randomhouse**.co.uk
www.**rbooks**.co.uk

Addresses for companies within The Random House Group Limited
can be found at: www.randomhouse.co.uk/offices.htm

THE RANDOM HOUSE GROUP Limited Reg. No. 954009

A CIP catalogue record for this book is available from the British Library.

CONTENTS

Dedicated to anyone
who has ever been
The New Girl or Boy

EIGHTEEN MOONS
OF WITCH BABY

'Hello? Anybody home?'

Silence greeted the postman standing on the front doorstep of Arkon House. He cleared his throat and tried again.

'Er. HellooOOO. Postie. Got a p-p-p-p-parcel for you.'

He was beginning to sound like a mad owl. He finished with a sort of youOoOoOoOoOo$_u$ sound that trailed away into the silence.

The postman swallowed. Hard.

If only there had been a letterbox in the front door of Arkon House, he could have posted the parcel through its slot and that would have been the end of it. However, with no letterbox, the postman had to hand over the parcel to whoever was on the other side of the door. And the problem with *that* was he'd heard that

Arkon House was haunted — and not by any old **Woo-hoo**, icy-fingers-running-up-and-down-your-spine kind of ghost, but by an ancient ghoul with nasty habits and a particular fondness for eating postmen.

Earlier that morning, back at the post office, the idea of a postman-munching monster sounded ridiculous, but now he wasn't so sure. Now, the postman wanted to dump the parcel and run away as fast as his legs could carry him. However, all postmen are taught that, come rain, hail or monsters, The Mail Must Get Through.

One last try, he decided, *then I'm out of here.*

Although it didn't have a letterbox, the front door of Arkon House did have a huge brass knocker in the shape of a toad, so the postman seized this and rapped it sharply

against the door with a loud **rat-a-tat-tat**.

As the Toad told her Sisters while the three witches were eating supper that evening, *this* was exactly the kind of dumb mistake humans were always making.

'Stuck his grubby fingers up my nostrils and rapped my rear end *three* times on the door!' she croaked, her eyes goggling at the memory.

The Nose and the Chin ~~tsssked~~ in sympathy.

'I mean, what else was I supposed to do?' the Toad continued, hopping backwards and forwards across the tabletop where the three Sisters of Hiss were having supper. 'My bum *still* hurts.'

'Too much information,' muttered the Chin, spearing a lump of gristle on her plate* and flicking it onto the floor. A small black cat

* So sharp is the Chin's chin, she could easily have used it to spear the lump of gristle instead of her fork.

appeared from the shadows, pounced on this morsel and devoured it. The three Sisters gazed at the cat fondly.

'I actually think that turning him into a cat was a brilliant idea,' said the Nose, bending down* to make the kind of encouraging noises that cats are supposed to enjoy: 'Heeeere, possty wossty, psspsspss chhhhhh – who's a ssssweet pussy wussy?'

'Oh, give me strength,' the Chin said under her breath, adding in a normal voice, 'Changing people into animals is all very well, but we haven't worked out how to change them back. Have we, Toad dear?'

The Toad ignored this, running her tongue round her empty plate in the hope of finding an overlooked crumb.

* So big is the Nose's nose, she had to be extra careful that she didn't bang it on the floor as she bent down.

'Look,' the Chin said, 'I've told you before: no more magic spells. They're too dangerous. We're living here, surrounded by humans. We're trying to pretend that we are dear little old ladies. Harmless, toothless and utterly forgettable. If we keep on spelling willy-nilly, sooner or later a human will notice that we're "different", and then we'll be in deep poo.'

The Toad rolled her eyes and yawned.

'DEEP POO,' the Chin repeated. 'It's only been a few hundred years since they barbecued the last witch in Scotland. If they did it then, they can do it again. So. No more magic unless it's absolutely necessary. It's too dangerous.'

'Hang on a minute,' shrilled the Nose. 'If we're not allowed to do any magic, then just *what* exactly are we going to eat?'

The Sisters looked down at their plates.

'Suddenly I'm not hungry,' whispered the Toad, remembering what supper had been before she'd turned it into supper.*

'We don't need magic to make supper,' the Chin said. 'The Toad is perfectly capable of making a good wholesome meal out of whatever she can find lying around—'

'Hang on a minute,' interrupted the Nose. 'I think you're forgetting that we're *witches*, dear Sisters, and not just any old witches either. *We* are the **Sisters of HiSS**. Magic is part of what makes us Us. It is like the very air we breathe.

* Before the Toad's spell, supper was three scabby rats that she had found next to the dustbins. Three rats plus assorted thistles, nettles and pondweed. Grusomely, the rats were already long dead when the Toad found them. So long dead that bits of them had come back to life again.

We cannot live without it. It is as natural—'

'Yes, yes, yes,' interrupted the Chin. 'Fascinating. But all the same, no more magic unless it's strictly necessary. Changing that innocent postman into a pussycat was a really stupid use of magic.'

'**MeeyOwl**,' agreed the innocent postman.

'That was a spur-of-the-moment spell,' the Toad said. 'It won't happen again. I'm really, really sorry.'

'What?' the postman squeaked in Cat. 'Is that it? Sorry? You're *sorry*? Have you any idea just how sorry *I* am? What about **meeeeeeyOwl**?'

The Sisters ignored him.

'Now,' said the Chin, 'there's a full moon tonight, which means our baby is exactly eighteen full moons old.'

'**Witch Baby**!' squealed the Toad, hopping up and down with excitement. 'Our dear little adopted human child. To think that she's already eighteen months old. Seems like only yesterday when we chose her at the hospital. Oh, she's soooo sweet and small . . . I *so* wish we didn't have to wait until she's big before—'

'**Ughhhh**,' interrupted the Nose, '*babies*. Disgusting, dribbly little beasts. Who'd be a human parent? I can't tell you how glad I am that *we* don't have to raise her. Nappies? Fluffy toys? Fairy stories?'

'I love fairy stories,' whispered the Toad. 'Especially the one where the Toad gets kissed by the handsome prince—'

Once upon a time there was a very pretty ~~princess.~~ frog

'You're going soft in the head,' said the Nose: 'a) it's a *frog*, and b) it gets kissed by a beautiful *princess*.'

'Don't care,' muttered the Toad. '*And* I don't care if we agreed not to get Witch Baby till she's bigger. I don't want to wait any longer. I want to go and get her right now.'

'Oh, pu**h-leaze**,' groaned the Chin. 'How many times do I have to say this? *We* aren't going to raise Witch Baby. Her human parents will do that for us. Then, when the time is right, we'll step in and take over. And *not* one moment before. Do I make myself plain?'

The Toad didn't reply. Instead, she slid off the table onto a chair and then dropped to the floor with a small **thud**.

11

'I only wanted a little baby to hug,' she said, waddling towards the kitchen. '*I* don't mind nappies, fluffy toys and stories.' Outside the window, the full moon rose for the eighteenth time since Witch Baby had arrived on Earth. The Toad heaved a sigh. In a house only three minutes on a broomstick away, Witch Baby would be getting ready for bed. The Toad sighed again.

Nappies, fluffy toys and fairy tales? How hard could that be?

One :

My smelly little sister

I tell you, babies are *hard* work. Right now, baby Daisy MacRae is probably the wettest, stickiest, smelliest baby on planet Earth. She is also my baby sister and, sadly, to earn more pocket money, I have promised to do the needful with Daisy's nappy every night before she has her bath.

Tonight her nappy is **gruesome**. Tonight even Mum turned pale when she passed Daisy over to me.

'Soddy, Lid,' she said, holding her nose with one hand as she fanned the air in front of her face with the other. 'Daidy smeds preddy awfud.'

Mum's not kidding. Daisy smells *awful*. If I smelled like that, I'd flush myself down

the toilet. But Daisy doesn't care what she smells like. Daisy thinks her nappy is hilarious.

'Hahahaha POO,' she roars, running down the corridor. 'POO, POO, smelly smellysmelly,' she says proudly, adding, 'Getta BAFF.'

Too right. Get a bath right now. Unfortunately, this is not as easy as it sounds. The trick with Daisy is to turn her bath times into a sort of wet playtime. As long as she thinks we're playing *Lily and Daisy's Wonderful Bath Game*, she'll do just about anything I want her to do. However, the minute she realizes I'm trying to speed her into the bath and out the other side into her pyjamas and then (whisper it) *Off to Bee-Ee-Dee*, that's when the trouble starts.

Problem is, Daisy isn't a normal kind of baby baby. My little sister is **Something Else Entirely**. I call her a Witch Baby because I can't think what else to call her.* Daisy is a Witch Baby because ever since she was born

---

* That's not exactly true. Yesterday, when I found her drawing on my pillow with my brand new marker pens, I could think of lots of things to call her. And then, when she got bored drawing with my pens and turned them into raspberry liquorice snakes and ate them, I thought of even more things to call her. Come to think of it, that's probably why Daisy's nappy stinks. Eating raspberry liquorice snakes can't be good for a Witch Baby's tummy.

she could do magic. Real, proper magic spells. Spells like the one when she put my head on the wrong way round or turned me into a slug. Once, memorably, she even changed my big brother Jack and me into vampires.

Fortunately, I've learned a few things about Daisy's spells. For instance, she can only do one spell at a time. This might be because she's only very little; maybe when she's bigger, she'll be able to do lots at once, but for now it's one at a time.

Thank heavens.

Also her spells can be broken if she is distracted. If I make her laugh, or if she bursts into tears or finds something more interesting to do, then . . . **Pfffff**, the spell fades.

Thank goodness.

As you can imagine, I spend an awful lot of time worrying about whether Daisy is about to do a spell, and I can't even relax when she *isn't* doing spells because that's when she conjures up her magical dog WayWoof. No spells equals WayWoof.

Speaking of which . . . there she is, Daisy's very own, home-spelled witchy pet, WayWoof, with her tail waving and tongue flopping out of one side of her mouth as she lollops towards us.

Hi, WayWoof. Yes. Yes. NO. **Eughhhh**. Don't sniff *that*. It's a nappy. A *used* nappy. **Oh, gag**.

WayWoof looks like a normal dog, but she's not. Two things make her completely different from other dogs.

One: she smells. Yes, I know, all dogs smell; sort of woolly, meaty and *doggy*, but WayWoof *really* smells. Imagine the pong of a dustbin plus a gas leak and add the whiff of stinky cheese, then multiply all that by ten and *that's* WayWoof.

Two: WayWoof f a d e s away when Daisy begins to concentrate on a spell. This is very useful, because it's like a kind of early-warning-Daisy-spell alert.

Three: I know, I said *two* things about WayWoof, but I forgot the most important one. WayWoof is invisible. Except that's not *exactly* true. I can see WayWoof, Daisy can see WayWoof, my best friend Vivaldi can see her,[*] other dogs can see her, but that's it.

---

[*] I'll explain why in a minute . . .

Everyone else thinks the smell is me. Especially my big brother, Jack. Every time a bad smell wafts up his nostrils, he assumes that it came from me.

Except right now. When Daisy runs into Jack's bedroom wearing the **NAPPY OF NASTINESS**, even Jack can work out that the stench comes from Daisy, not me. He looks up from the music magazine he's reading, sighs mightily, removes one earbud from his ear and

looks around as if he's not quite sure where he is. Jack always looks like this. His nose twitches, then wrinkles up like a walnut.

'**Phwoarrrr**,' he says. 'Daiseeeee. Was that you?'

'No, Dack,' lies my little sister. 'WayWoof smelly. No Daisy. Lillil smelly. No Daisy. Dack smelly. Hahahahaha . . .'

But fortunately, Jack isn't listening any more. Tss, tss. Jack's put his earbud back in – tss, tss – and now he can't hear Daisy, even though he can still smell her.

Oh, sigh. Now WayWoof has followed Daisy into the bathroom and is happily drinking water out of the toilet while Daisy hurls Barbies into the bath.

'LIIIILLLLEEEEEE?' Mum yells from downstairs. 'Is Daisy even *in* the bath yet? You'll have to get a move on – tomorrow's a Big Day.'

Thanks for reminding me, Mum. As if I could forget. Tomorrow is a huge day. Tomorrow is my first day at a new school. Just thinking about this makes my tummy feel weird. We moved house at the beginning of the summer holidays; moved house, friends, school, city, Dad's job . . . everything. A big red removal van swallowed everything from our old home in Edinburgh and hauled it up to our new house here in the Highlands.

At first it was horrible. I missed all my old friends and I missed our old house. However, because we'd moved at the start of the summer holidays, I didn't really miss my old school. But now that the holidays are over and it's back-to-school time, I'm feeling really nervous because I'm not going to my old school in Edinburgh. Tomorrow I'm starting at a tiny little school where *everyone's* in the same class. How weird is *that*? And it's not only me who has to start at a new school. Daisy's starting playgroup. And guess where her playgroup is? Next door to my new class in my new school.

That means there's no escape. Much as I love my little sister (and I do – I love her to bits), she is HARD WORK. Every time I'm out with her, I worry that somebody will notice that she's not exactly 'normal'. Actually, I'm amazed that no one's spotted Daisy's weird witchy ways yet. Most grown-ups hardly notice *anything*, even if it's going on right under their noses.

Thank goodness.

Imagine if we'd lived four hundred years ago. Back then they used to *kill* anyone they suspected of being a 𝔴𝔦𝔱𝔠𝔥. Nowadays they'd probably make a TV programme about them. And how embarrassing would *that* be? The whole world would know about my little Witch Baby sister. Right now, the only other person who knows that Daisy has 𝔰𝔭𝔢𝔠𝔦𝔞𝔩 powers is my friend, Vivaldi.*

Vivaldi is the only person I'll know at my new school. My big brother Jack says that there's nothing special about being born under a Blue

---

* Vivaldi and I have the same birthday - she's the only other person in the whole world that I've ever met who was born under a Blue Moon, just like me (she's also the only other person who knows Daisy is a witch). This is supposed to give us both Special Powers too. So far, our Special Powers have only resulted in our being able to see Way-Woof. Not that Special, really. Not very Powerful, either.

Moon like Vivaldi and me, but he's wrong. He can't see WayWoof and he doesn't notice when Daisy casts a spell – he wouldn't notice if a volcano erupted in his bath. Poor Jack.

Talking of baths . . . Daisy has climbed into ours, even though I haven't run it yet. She's sitting in our big empty bath with a long

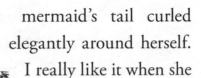

mermaid's tail curled elegantly around herself. I really like it when she does this kind of fishy spell; it's the reason I don't mind giving her a bath at night. She isn't always a mermaid; sometimes she's a Daisy-seal or even a shoal of Daisy-fish. Tonight her mermaid's tail is covered in pale pink scales and she's given herself long lilac hair.

I think she looks amazing, but I'm not entirely sure her playgroup leader would agree. Daisy the mermaid is talking to herself and her Barbies as if she's the mummy and they're her family. She has no idea that she's starting at playgroup tomorrow. My tummy gives one of those sort of backflips that happen when I'm really nervous.

Mum is right. Tomorrow is a Very Big Day.

Two:

Pants to that

'Just like one big happy family,' Dad said at breakfast on the Very Big Day.

'Happy?' snorted Jack in a sort of disbelieving way. 'What's so happy about families?'

Daisy agreed with Dad, though. '**Happyappyappyappy**,' she bawled, stabbing a bit of toast into her yoghurt and mashing the whole mess into her hair.

'Euughhh. Daisy. That is *disgusting*,' Mum said. 'Stop. STOP. No. Don't rub it in.'

'*I* went to a very small school,' Dad continued, ignoring Daisy's bread-and-yoghurt head massage. 'All of us in one classroom. Never did me any harm. You're going to love it, Lily.'

'Luvvit, luvvit, Lily,' Daisy echoes as Mum hauls her off to the bathroom.

Jack shudders and puts his earbuds in. Tsss, tsss, TSSSS. Lucky him. His school doesn't start till next week, whereas Daisy and I start today. Suddenly I'm not hungry any more. I wonder – if I rubbed bread and yoghurt in my hair, would Mum let me off school? Probably not.

Dad sees my face and comes over to give me a huge hug. 'Come on, flower,' he says. 'By tonight you'll be wondering what all the fuss was about. By tonight it won't be a new school any more. It'll be *your* school. Things are rarely as bad as you imagine they'll be. Honest. You'll have a great time.'

An hour later, standing outside the new school and trying to ignore WayWoof running around in circles, I'm hoping Dad's right. However, despite his cheery advice, I feel as if I'm about to be eaten by monsters; as if a volcano is about to erupt beneath my feet; as if there's a meteorite rushing towards planet Earth and I'm standing right where it's going to hit.

'Right, Lily,' Mum says in her let's-be-cheerful-even-if-we're-being-gnawed-by-piranhas voice. 'I'll just take Daisy in to playgroup and stay with her for a bit. You'll be all right, won't you?'

Er. I look around. Sadly there are no monsters, erupting volcanoes or falling meteorites heading my way. No. It's far worse. There's a group of strange children and their parents. And WayWoof.

'Um. Yes. I'll be fine,' I say in a strangled voice that doesn't sound like me at all.

Mum smiles. 'I know it's early days, but let's hope playgroup will be good for Daisy

and that she'll make some friends . . .'
Then she notices that Daisy's already
started making friends. My Witch
Baby's down on her hands and knees,
growling softly to herself and patting
the shoes of a little boy
who looks as if he's
about to faint
with terror.
Somehow, I
don't think
this is what
Mum meant.

'Stop it, Daisy,' Mum hisses. 'Leave his laces
alone.'

Daisy smiles at me.

Uh-oh.

I know that smile.

And WayWoof is fading fast.

Uh-oh. Incoming Spell Alert.

Daisy? I look down. The little boy's shoelaces are whipping backwards and forwards as if they're angry. Now they're slipping out of his shoes like twin snakes.

Oh *no*.

They *are* twin snakes. Before this goes any further, I have to distract Daisy from her spell. If I don't, *anything* might happen. The snakes might bite. They might wind themselves round the little boy's legs and strangle his ankles. I have to do something right *now*, before it's too late.

'Daisy. Look!' I yell, flinging myself onto my hands and turning a cartwheel. 'LOOK, DAISY!' I bawl. 'See if you can tell what colour my pants are—'

Yes. I know. I was desperate. If I'd really thought it through, of *course* I would never have done such a stupid thing.

'Lily. For heaven's sake,' Mum hisses, 'be*HAVE*.'

I stand up. I've just spotted WayWoof sloping out from behind the school's wheelie bins. Phew. If WayWoof's back, then Daisy isn't doing her snake spell any more.

'Pink,' says Daisy firmly.

'No they weren't,' says a familiar voice.

Oh NO.

'Your big sister's pants are blue,' the voice continues, making me want to die of embarrassment. It's my one and only friend, Vivaldi. At least, she *was* my one and only friend until five seconds ago. But now, after the pants-in-the-air incident, she'll probably fade out of my life even faster than WayWoof does when Daisy's Up To No Good.

'However,' Vivaldi continues, '*my* pants are purple with yellow stars.' And to my relief, my brilliant, loyal and slightly mad friend turns three cartwheels to prove her point.

Mum's eyes are out on stalks, but Daisy is laughing like a drain. The little boy with the laces takes one look at us and flees into the school. From somewhere in the building a bell rings.

Time to go. My first day at my new school is off to a flying start.

Three:

In with a hiss

'School?' The Nose's voice climbs to a shriek. 'Whatever are they thinking of?'

The Toad doesn't reply. She's poring over a recipe book, trying to find a new and tasty way to cook rats and nettles. Until the Sisters of Hiss come to grips with the Internet or work out how to drive to the nearest shop, nettles and rats are all there is to eat.

'I *said*,' hissed the Nose, 'whatever are they thinking of?'

There is a loud and exasperated hiss from the other side of the room, and the Chin's face appears round the side of her computer monitor.

'What is it *now*?' she demands, her tone waspish, her eyes shrunk down to two little slits of menace. The Chin is completely fed up. Two hours of struggling with the computer have put her in a foul mood.

'School,' the Nose repeats. 'They're sending *our* Witch Baby to school. They're idiots. **MORONS**. Nitty-witty pea-brained fruit **LOOPS**!'

'Calm down,' the Toad mutters. 'There's no point in getting hysterical. You'll only end up doing something awful.'

From over by the fireplace comes a plaintive meow. The postman-cat agrees with the Toad. He knows all about the awful things a hysterical witch can do.

'But . . . but . . . you don't under*stand*,' the Nose wails. 'If our little Witch Baby goes to school, she'll learn all sorts of rubbish. That's what they teach at human school. Rubbish. Her head will be stuffed full of twiddle-twaddle and then it'll take us *years* to unstuff it before we can even begin to teach her anything useful.'

'Mmmm-hmm,' agrees the Chin, but you can tell that she hasn't really been paying attention. In fact, the Chin is only aware of what is on her computer screen. Somehow, she's finally found her way onto the website for a major supermarket. At long last there'll be something other than rats and nettles for supper.

'Yesssss!' she squeaks, typing in the word 'chocolate' when the computer asks what she would like to buy. Just for fun, she types in the number 13 when it asks how many deluxe boxes of Swiss chocolate she would like delivered to Arkon House.

There is a beep as thirteen hugely expensive and delicious boxes of chocolate are added to her online shopping basket. In the background, the Chin is dimly aware of the Nose rattling on and on about teachers and schools and Witch Baby. The Chin nods, but she's not listening. Instead, she's tapping in the magic number 13 in answer to the question of how many

12-portion cheese-and-pepperoni pizzas with extra chillies she would like delivered. The Chin has no idea what a pizza or a chilli might be, but because she's a witch, she loves the idea of a food that looks like the full moon.

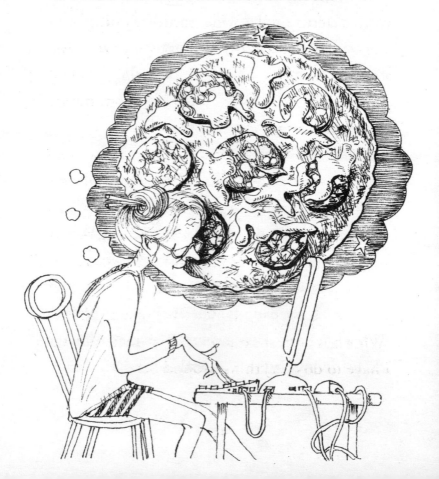

By the time the Nose has finally finished her rant, the Chin is triumphantly pressing the 'enter' key to complete her online shopping order.

'There,' she says, sitting back in her chair with a terrifyingly wide smile running like a gash straight across her face. 'That's *that* settled.'

'Really?' the Nose squeaks. 'You mean, you're quite *happy* about going in?'

The Chin's forehead wrinkles up in accordion pleats. Whatever is the Nose talking about? 'Going in?' she asks.

'Yes,' the Nose explains. 'To the school. To keep an eye on our Witch Baby. You *know*. Go in and pretend to work at the school.'

The Chin is somewhat taken aback. 'Wh-wh-what?' she quavers, 'Why me? Why do I have to do everything around here?'

'Because,' the Nose says wearily, 'toads don't, as a general rule, get jobs in schools, and I can't read or write.* So *you* have to go to school.'

'But . . .' the Chin begins, but she knows the Nose is right. One of them has to make sure that playgroup doesn't turn their Witch Baby back into a human baby.

'But how will you tell?' the Toad enquires, closing her recipe book with a sigh. There *are* no good recipes for rats and nettles.

'Tell what?' the Nose says.

* Poor Nose. Somehow she never got around to learning how to read and write. When she was a Witch Baby, people were too busy learning how to catch their supper or avoid *being* supper for a sabre-toothed tiger to bother with anything like inventing books.

'How will you tell if our Witch Baby's being turned into a human bean?' the Toad asks, adding, 'I mean, what are the first signs of bean-brain?'

'There are three main things to watch out for,' the Nose begins. 'One: humans watch television in the afternoon. Two:—'

'Hang *on*,' the Toad squeaks. '*You* watch television in the afternoon—'

'That's different,' snaps the Nose. 'That's research. You don't think I'm doing it for *fun*, do you? Now shut up and let me finish. Two: humans love to drink sweet fizzy liquids, although why this is so I fail to understand; and Three: humans love to eat that hideous stringy flatbread stuff. Oh, what's it called? Pits? Pat's? Pete's?'

'Pizza?' says the Chin. 'I think I've just ordered thirteen of them on the computer. I had no *idea* they were so dangerous. Oh, well. Never mind. We can always feed them to the cat.'

'But . . . what will you do,' asks the Toad, 'if you find our Witch Baby being taught to eat pizza washed down with fizzy liquid in front of a television in the afternoon? What then?'

'Then?' says the Nose. 'That's easy. I'll call up a Vortex of Vanishment spell, and cause the school, the teachers and all the children except for our little Witch Baby to de-exist.'

At this, the Toad gulps and lowers her eyes to her recipe book. The Chin turns whiter than lemon yoghurt and quavers, 'Th-th-that does seem a *little* harsh, sister dear.'

'HARSH?' shrills the Nose. 'Tampering with a Witch Baby's destiny is a bad, bad thing,' she insists. 'What possible use is there for a TV-watching, pop-swilling, pizza-pigging witch? Hmmm? Where's the mystery? Where's the history? We're the **Sisters of HiSS**, not the *Sissies of Fizz*. We are as old as the hills, as permanent as the mountains and as wise as the—'

'All right, all right,' groans the Chin. 'Keep your wattles on. I'm going in. I'll make sure that our dearest little Witch Baby is unharmed by the evils of a twenty-first-century nursery. I'll keep her safe.' And with this, the Chin sweeps out of the door and off to school for the first time in hundreds of years.

Four:

The hairy eyeball in action

'Everybody? Let's say hello to Daisy, shall we?'

Miss McPhee has hold of one of Daisy's hands and WayWoof is nuzzling the other comfortingly. Not that Daisy needs comforting. Miss McPhee, her playleader, is lovely. She smells of flowers, has loads of wild red hair and wears big black boots. Daisy keeps gazing up at her in adoration, and is paying no attention to her new classmates. In front of Daisy are a dozen small children, none of whom are paying any attention to a Witch Baby and a WayWoof in their midst.

Hah. If only they knew what Daisy is really like, they'd run, shrieking, out of the classroom, far away from the school, and wouldn't stop until they reached John o' Groats. And if they knew what WayWoof really smells like, they'd jump into the sea at John o' Groats and wouldn't stop swimming till they reached Norway.

However, none of them know Daisy and WayWoof like I do, so all the small children carry on doing exactly what they were doing when Daisy and WayWoof arrived.

Daisy shuffles closer to Miss McPhee and turns to wave at me. 'Go 'way, Lillil. Ba-bye. See later, cockodile.'

'In a while, alligator,' I say, dreading what happens next.

Because next it's . . .

My New Classroom
by Lily MacRae

I open the door and there they are. A room full of staring strangers, among whom are three faces I recognize. Only one of the three is smiling. This is even worse than I'd imagined. I blink. It's Vivaldi smiling at me and patting the empty seat beside her. Standing by a desk on the other side of the room is Mrs McDonald, my new teacher.

Gulp. My legs begin to shake. *Smile, Lily*, I tell myself.

Mrs McDonald waves me in. 'Come away in, Lily dear,' she says. 'Now, everybody, let's welcome Lily to our school.'

One by one, the strangers stand up and introduce themselves. I smile and smile, but inside I'm thinking, **Aaaargh**, *when will this be over?*

'Hi, Lily, my name's Yoshito Harukashi.'

'Craig.'

'Hello, Lily, I'm Vivaldi's wee sister, Mozart.'

'Lily? Like the flower? Hmmm. We've met already. I'm James Nicholas Dunlop and this stinky haddock-breath here's—'

'Oh, shut *up*. I *can* speak for myself *actually*, Jamie. I'm his sister, Annabel. We met before. We came to your moving-in party in your tiny cottage. We're from Mishnish Castle.'

'Ah'm Shane and ah'm the oldest in the class.'

My head is spinning. We aren't even halfway round the class and already I'm getting them all mixed up. Thankfully, Vivaldi grabs my arm and hauls me onto the seat beside her.

'Nightmare, eh?' she mutters. 'Annabel never misses a chance to go on about her biiiig house and Shane always has to tell you that he's the oldest – basically because he's so small and weedy.'

Yoshito has her hand up. 'Can we make name badges, Mrs McDonald?' she asks. 'To help Lily remember who we are?'

Mrs McDonald considers Yoshito's idea for a moment, and in the silence we hear Craig say something very rude under his breath. Mrs McDonald turns round very slowly until she's facing Craig. Uh-oh.

'I didn't quite catch what you said, Craig dear. Care to repeat it?' Then she puts her head on one side, like a bird trying to decide whether to eat a worm.

Craig flushes bright red and folds his arms around his chest.

'Forgotten it?' Mrs McDonald asks.

Craig looks as if he's trying to make his head disappear down his neck, like a tortoise. In a barely audible voice he whispers, 'Aye.'

'Well, that's a shame,' says Mrs McDonald. 'Never mind. Can't have been too important, hmmm?'

Craig is staring at the floor and not looking up at Mrs McDonald.

Mrs McDonald smiles. 'Name badges. What a good idea, Yoshito. Let's start right away. And not another peep from you, Craig, hmmm?'

'No,' mutters Craig, then, 'No, Mrs McDonald.'

Craig hardly says another word, rude or otherwise, for the rest of the morning. And unlike my old teacher back in Edinburgh, Mrs McDonald doesn't roar or shout once. She doesn't even raise her voice. I think I'm going to really like her. She's the kind of teacher who makes you *want* to get along with her. Fierce but fair. She doesn't have to roar and shout; all she has to do is *look*[*] at you.

Mind you, when you're the new girl, *everyone* looks at you. Sneakily like Annabel (in the mirror over by the book corner, when she thinks I can't see), or creepily like Donald (he just stares and stares with an open mouth as if he's about to take a bite out of me), or even shyly like Yoshito, who turns pink if I smile back at her.

[*] Quelling your class with one look is a well-known Scottish teachers' skill which is called 'Gieing Them the Hairy Eyeball'. When a teacher turns his or her Hairy Eyeball on a misbehaving child, the eyeballee feels in turn: hot, cold, shaky, embarrassed and, finally, desperate to go to the bathroom.

But Shane doesn't look at me. Not once all morning. In fact, he acts as if I'm not there, which is pretty rude. Shane's friend Craig is rude too, but he's also horrible to the little ones in our class. When he thinks Mrs McDonald can't see him, he makes faces behind their backs, sticks his foot out to trip them up and nudges them so that they drop stuff. He's so huge that nobody dares to say anything back to him.

We're supposed to be making name badges, which would take me about five minutes at home, but here at school it's taking for ever.

'Mrs McDonald,' Jamie says, 'I need a bigger bit of card for my badge. I can't fit all my names onto this one.'

Vivaldi rolls her eyes at me.

'Just leave some of them out,' suggests

Mozart. '*I* had to. Or else write them in wee writing.'

'*WEE* writing?' snorts Shane. '**Yeeeurchhh**. Jamie's writing in wee, Jamie's writing in w—'

'Shane *dear*,' sighs Mrs McDonald, and Shane slumps back in his chair.

Vivaldi writes **What an idiot** in pencil on her badge and immediately rubs it out before Mrs McDonald sees. Yoshito saw, though. She's holding her mouth and turning pink, and she looks as if she's about to explode with trying not to laugh out loud. I have to look away, or else I'm going to start laughing hysterically too. It's not even all *that* funny, either. It's just that I'm so nervous about this first day at school that it wouldn't take much to make me laugh, or scream or even burst into tears.

This must be what it felt like the very first

time I started school, when I was tiny. I can't remember much about it, except Mum said I clung to her knees and cried and cried for ever. Obviously I didn't do *that* this morning. For one thing, I would have had to lie down in the playground to get my arms round Mum's knees. And for another, I'm nine and a quarter years old, and clinging to my mum and begging her to take me home is . . . well, it's *not* going to help me make friends. So I'm very, very grateful that Vivaldi is here today. With her as my friend guiding me through the first few weeks, I might just about survive without making a complete idiot of myself.

Five:

Burning down the house

Although I really wanted to stick to Vivaldi like glue, at break time I had to go and check that Daisy was all right. After all, this was her very first time *ever* away from Mum. I couldn't work out whether this would make her even more of a witch than usual, or if it would calm her down. So, apologizing to Vivaldi, I rushed outside to check that Daisy *hadn't* turned everyone in her playgroup into worms, or worse. I found her in the little nursery play area, wandering in and out of the Wendy house with WayWoof behind her. Phew. Thank heavens for WayWoof.

The little boy whose laces Daisy had untied was devotedly trailing behind her and Way-Woof. Occasionally she would turn round and

flash him the kind of smile that should have a
health warning attached to it. Something like

STAND CLEAR, HUMAN.
LIVE WITCH.
DO NOT, REPEAT NOT, APPROACH.

You'd think the little boy would want to

avoid She-who-turns-laces-into-snakes, but like most of the victims of Daisy's spells, he has forgotten what she did to him. He hasn't been put off her at all. He faithfully shadows her round the tractor-tyre sandpit, past the climbing frame and the pirate ship, following her every step.

Now they're running round the outside edge of the nursery playground, weaving in and out of the trees and making **neeeeee-yowwwww** noises like aeroplanes. At least, I think that's what the little boy is doing. I happen to know that Daisy isn't pretending to be an aeroplane. She's not going **neeeeee-yowwwww**, she's going **rrrrroarrrrr** because I taught her how last week.[*]

While Daisy and her new friend are being very loud aeroplanes and dragons, WayWoof is having a great time; sniffling, snuffling and bounding up to tiny children and bouncing around them. As far as I can see, none of them can see WayWoof, but I can tell that all of them can smell her. One by one, they shriek to a halt as if they've run into an invisible glass wall.

Then their noses wrinkle up in an expression of horror and they look all around to see if they can find the Source of the Stink. Since there's nobody there except Daisy and her new friend, everyone will be thinking, Phwoaarrr, you two smell awful.

[*] We were reading one of her favourite picture books: *What Noise Does a Noisy Oyster Make?* We'd done the octopus page (*schleppa, schleppa, squeeeeeeeeze hug*) and the giraffe page (*hack, hack, cough, cough*) when Daisy turned to me and said, 'Daggon? What noise makes a daggon, Lil?' and off the top of my head I said, very loudly, '*Rrrrrrroarrrrrrrrr.*' She burst out laughing.

Poor Daisy. Poor little laces-as-snakes boy too. So unfair. Especially when they didn't make the smell and it was . . .

Uh-oh. WayWoof's gone.

Oh, help. Spell Alert. What's Daisy up to? I can't see her – *or* the little boy either. Maybe they've gone into the Wendy ho—

'**Neeeeeee-yowWwwww.**'

'**RrrrrrrOOOAAARRRRRRRRRRR!**'

I'm getting a bad feeling. The windows of

the Wendy house suddenly turn bright yellow, as if something very bright or very hot is happening inside – I'm running now, as fast as I can, straight into Daisy's new friend, who is showing every sign of being a small boy in urgent need of the bathroom. Thank heavens. That way he'll never have to see the vast, snorting, fire-breathing, tail-whipping thing that my dear little Witch Baby sister has turned herself into.

In the distance I hear a bell ring. It's probably the bell to let us know that playtime is over, but right now, all I can think about is how I'm going to survive the next few minutes without being barbecued by my little sister. Inside the Wendy house, it's hotter than the middle of a bonfire. In the centre is a very small, red-hot dragon wearing a furious scowl. At least, I *think* that's what its expression means, but I don't know

much about dragons; for all I know, this one may be feeling blissfully happy. It's squatting on top of a plastic mushroom with its wings folded tightly across its chest and little snorts of steam puffing out of
its nostrils.

It's also wearing one of Daisy's hairbands wrapped round one ear.

'Daisy?' I gasp.

Two vast jets of flame whoosh out of the dragon's nostrils and roll across the floor towards me with near-deadly accuracy.

Uh-oh. Obviously *not* feeling too Daisy-ish right now. 'HEY!' I squeak. 'Come ON, Squirt. I'm on *your* side. Don't *do* that.'

'Not squirt,' Daisy-the-dragon mutters, but the flames are sort of reverse-sucked back into her nostrils. Phew. I'm boiling hot, but at least I'm not grilled.

'What's wrong?' I say in my best don't-roast-me-I'm-family kind of voice.

The dragon flicks her tail backwards and forwards impatiently. I try not to notice that it makes a loud snapping **CRACK** every time it straightens out. Just like a whip. **Gulp**.

'Come on . . .' I say, as kindly as possible. 'Tell me. Perhaps I can make it better?'

'Not kissit better,' the dragon says firmly.

'Don't worry. I wouldn't dare to try and kiss it better,' I say. 'What's the matter? Where's your new friend? Come on, Daisy, let's see if we can find him.' Out of the corner of my eye I can see a faint dog-shaped cloud forming beside the Wendy-house door. This is very good news. If I can almost-but-not-quite make out WayWoof's outline, then Daisy's dragon spell must be fading.

'Not come on. Not wantit find friend. Want go home. Want MUMMA.'

Well. That's clear enough, but Mum's long gone. I happen to know that she went home to paint the kitchen and won't be back to pick up Daisy until lunch time. Help. What am I supposed to do with a small dragon that wants its mummy?

'Want MUMMA!' Daisy repeats, and at the same time she grows several metres in all directions until the whole of the Wendy house is full of hot, cross dragon. I am squashed into a corner, trying to avoid the huge flames pouring out of Daisy's nose as she bawls for her mummy: 'WANT MUMMA, WANT MY MUMMA,' and the flames go Snort, Whoomph in agreement.

In the intense heat, the roof is beginning to melt. Any minute now it'll fall in and everyone will see that there's a *dragon* standing next to me. Then they'll notice that the Wendy house is wrecked and then we'll be in real trouble, and nobody'll believe me when I say none of this is *my* fault. It's not *my* fault that we had to move house and I had to move school. It's not *my* fault that my little sister is a witch, and it's not *my* fault that the end-of-playtime bell has just rung and I'm stuck in a STUPID Wendy house with a GRUMPY DRAGON. My eyes are going all blurry and my nose is prickling and, to my horror, I think I might be about to cry . . .

. . . and then a little hand pats my arm.

'Not kye, Lillil. Poor

Lillil, **ahhhh**.' And Daisy wraps her chubby little arms around my knees and gives me a hug. Then, on the off-chance that Daisy's hug hadn't made me feel a hundred per cent better, WayWoof appears, lollops into the Wendy house, licks my hand and then releases the worst stench *ever*. **WOW**. Phew. Gasp. Daisy's back.

Six:

Not another squawk

That afternoon, the Chin is hiding in the hedge
outside the little school where Witch Baby has
just spent her first morning learning how to
be human. The Chin isn't enjoying the hedge
one single bit, and to make matters worse,
every so often a bird lands on a twig next to
where she is perched and picks a fight with her.

Despite promising to use magic only when it was absolutely necessary, the Chin decided that turning herself into a sparrow was a stroke of genius, but now . . .

Now she's not so sure. Now there's an enormous blackbird hopping from foot to foot in front of her and reading her the Riot Act.

'Aaark, awwwk TWEE,' the blackbird squawks. 'Tweedle, twirp TWEEET.'

'ShhhHHHHhhhh,' the Chin hisses, because she's trying not to attract any attention to herself, especially now that there are people coming out of Witch Baby's school.

'Aaark, TWEEP,' the blackbird shrieks. 'Twitter, twee, aaaAARRRGHHHHH?'

There's a puff of smoke, and a little cloud of black feathers drifts slowly to the ground. The blackbird has gone, and in its place,

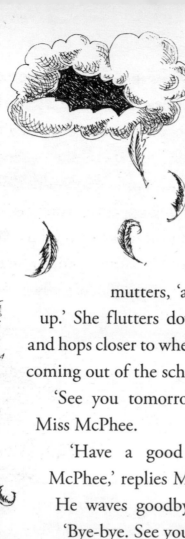

wriggling under the hedge, is a very confused-looking worm.

'One more squawk out of you,' the Chin mutters, 'and I'll gobble you up.' She flutters down to the ground and hops closer to where two humans are coming out of the school's back door.

'See you tomorrow, Mr Fox,' says Miss McPhee.

'Have a good afternoon, Miss McPhee,' replies Mr Fox, the janitor. He waves goodbye to her, calling, 'Bye-bye. See you tomorrow, bright and early.'

Not if I can help it, the Chin decides, identifying Miss McPhee as the nursery teacher and hopping after her. Poor Miss McPhee doesn't notice the weird-looking sparrow following her until it's too late. She is halfway down Blackthorn Lane when the Chin strikes. There's a stifled squeak, a small thud as Miss McPhee falls to the ground, and suddenly, where there was only one sparrow, there are now two.

'Eh?' Miss McPhee squawks, her beak wide open in shock. 'What? Whooo? What on earth are *these*? WINGS?' And, feathers fluttering, she keels over sideways in a dead faint.

There's a victorious cackle and the air shivers as the Chin turns back into an old lady with a chin as sharp as a meathook. Checking that Blackthorn Lane is still deserted, the Chin plucks the unfortunate Miss McPhee-sparrow off the ground, tucks the limp bird under her shawl and sets off for Arkon House as fast as her legs can carry her.

That night, the Chin is still hard at work. Shadows cast by the light of her computer screen dance round the walls of the Sisters' living room. Over by the sulking fire, the Nose is dozing, and in the kitchen the Toad is still carefully licking the supper dishes clean.

'There,' says the Chin, rubbing her eyes and yawning hideously. Over by the fire, the Nose wakes with a snort, tries to disguise this as a cough and ends up choking and gagging so much that she puts the fire out.

'Oh, for the love of toadspawn,' mutters

the Chin. However, she's too delighted with her own cleverness to allow anything to dampen her enthusiasm. 'I've just given myself a job at our little Witch Baby's school,' she continues, tapping a couple of keys on her computer. 'In a few days I'm taking over from Miss McPhee.'

In a rusty birdcage on the other side of the room, the real Miss McPhee flaps her feathers and swears in Sparrow.

On the floor beneath her cage, the postman-cat miaows in agreement. The Chin ignores them both and continues gleefully, 'Tomorrow, the school will receive an e-mail telling them that, unfortunately, Miss McPhee has been called away to look after her sister and will therefore not be able to come to school. In her place, the Education Department are sending a temporary replacement – TA-DAAA – me! Miss Chin.'

The Nose nods slowly. 'Y…e…e…e…s,' she agrees, 'that sounds pretty good. Nice touch about looking after her sister, by the way. Whatever gave you that idea?'

The Chin smiles nastily. 'I was thinking about how I look after *my* Sisters and how nice it would be if *they* looked after *me* for a change. You didn't think I was going to do *all* the work round here, did you?'

The Nose's face falls. There's something about the Chin's tone that bodes ill. The Nose is beginning to get a bad feeling about what's coming next. 'Er . . .' she bleats.

'Precisely,' the Chin snaps. 'So. My plan – and I have to say that I think it's a very good plan – is that you should *make* some money. Not too much. Just a couple of bin bags full. **Pfff**, let's start with a million pounds or so.'

'But . . . but . . .' The Nose is horrified. A million pounds? WHAT?

'And,' the Chin continues, ignoring the flappy, fluttery sounds now coming from the Nose, 'you'd better get a move on because the rent's due soon and I've just spent all the money we had on chocolate and pizza.'

'But . . . LISTEN!' the Nose squeals. 'I

have no *idea* how to make money. You know I can't read, and can barely count.'

The Chin rolls her eyes. 'So?' she sneers. 'I can't *teach*, but soon I'll start my job teaching children. The Toad can't *cook*, but she makes our supper every night. It's your turn. So what if you can't make money? You can *learn*. You'll pick it up as you go along. It can't be all that difficult. Most really rich people are pretty stupid anyway . . .'

The Nose has a sneaking suspicion that she's being insulted. '*What* are you saying?' she squeaks.

The Chin stands up and stretches. It's been a long, long day. 'I'm saying, *Get a job*.'

She yawns, heading for bed, and adds over her shoulder, 'And I'm saying Goodnight.'

As the Chin's footsteps fade into silence, the Nose is almost sure she can hear her sister cackling quietly as she goes upstairs.

Seven:

Storm warning

Dad was right. My new school isn't quite as bad as I thought it was going to be. Actually, it's OK with Vivaldi there. Before I really thought about it, I discovered that I was looking forward to Mondays (running), Tuesdays (art), Wednesdays (music), Thursdays (Sticky Toffee Pudding) and Fridays (project: weather).

I've only been here for a few days so I haven't really made friends with anyone else apart from Vivaldi. There are fourteen people in our class, and I'm still trying to learn everyone's names. Especially the names of the scary ones. Maybe they won't be horrible to me if I get their names right. Crane and Shake. NO! No, no, no. I *mean* Craig and Shane. Oh, help. Craig and Shane, the Wild Animals. Even though

Mrs McDonald got us to make and wear name badges on the first day, I still get muddled up. The pictures help, though. We all had to illustrate our badges with something that gave a hint about who we are.

Vivaldi drew a paintbrush on her badge, then she scored it out, stuck a piece of paper over it and drew a guitar instead.

'Go on, Lil' – she grinned – 'I dare you. Draw your bagpipes.'

My heart sank down to my knees. For one thing, bagpipes are *really* hard to draw, and for another, I'm really embarrassed to admit that I play them. But a dare's a dare, so I drew my pipes.

Just as I'd suspected, my name badge now looks like LILY (the SPIDER). Oh, sigh. But I think the badges are a great idea. I already know the names of at least five other people

in my class, and it's the pictures on the badges that help me remember who they are. There's Yoshito (the FISH), Jamie (the GUN), Annabel (the PONY), Donald (the TRACTOR) and Vivaldi's little sister, Mozart (the FAIRY).

I *have* met Annabel (the PONY)* and her brother Jamie (the GUN) before. When we first moved here from Edinburgh, Mum and Dad threw a big let's-meet-the-neighbours

---

* Her name badge should have shown a ROTTING FISH rather than a PONY. For some reason, Annabel's breath stinks. Really stinks.

  [What Lily doesn't know is that a month ago, the Sisters of Hiss magicked up a batch of bacteria-coated special crisps and sneaked them into the buffet at Lily's house-warming party. This act of culinary terrorism was designed to destroy the budding friendship between Lily and Vivaldi. Obviously it didn't work. Lily and Vivaldi didn't eat a single one of the special crisps. Annabel ate the entire bowlful and was promptly sick several times. The after-effect of eating the magically corrupted crisps was three months of bad breath. That's bad, as in 'baaaaad'.]

If she wasn't so horrible, I might feel sorry for her.

party and Jamie and Annabel came with their dad. Both of them were spectacularly sick, and had to go home early. Maybe that's why they're not very friendly. Jamie stares right through me as if I'm invisible, and Annabel has a very annoying habit of wrinkling up her nose and sighing every time I come near, as if I smell awful.* Fortunately I'm used to this because of WayWoof, who has followed Daisy to school every day and made everyone at school wrinkle up their noses.

Talking of WayWoof, I can hear her next door. She's barking her invisible head off. Nobody else can hear her except Vivaldi, Daisy and me, which is just as well because WayWoof is barking very loudly.

Arf arf AWoOoOoOOoOo.

Vivaldi frowns and turns to mouth, *What's going on?* at me. I can't reply because Mrs

---

* Weird, huh? Since it's her that smells bad, not me.

McDonald is writing on the whiteboard, and any minute now she'll spin round and start firing questions at us.

AWOOOOO?

I shrug and try to ignore WayWoof, but it's not easy. What on earth is the matter? I honestly don't think I've *ever* heard her bark before. WayWoof has to be the most laid-back dog in the whole world. You could burgle our house in broad daylight,

devour the contents of the fridge and make a bonfire out of all our furniture and WayWoof would yawn in your face, slump to the floor with a sigh, produce an *evil* stench and fall asleep. So why is she barking? Is something wrong with Daisy?

'Lily?'

Uh-oh. Mrs McDonald is staring straight at me.

'Dreaming, were you, Lily? Or lost in thought?' She flashes me a smile and taps the whiteboard behind her. 'Your thoughts on what we're discussing, please?'

YowWWwL arf, arf YIP, suggests WayWoof.

Help. What are we discussing? I scan the whiteboard behind her. There are several things written on it.

Weather Forecasting [it says]

How do we know when it's going to rain, snow or hail?

How do we predict sunshine, blizzards, thunderstorms, heatwaves, etc.?

Oh, dear. For a moment I have no idea. All I can think of is WayWoof, but Mrs McDonald is smiling, as if to say that *anything* I can come up with will be welcome, so I open my mouth and try my best.

'Er . . .' I can still hear WayWoof barking a warning, and suddenly I have my answer: '*Animals!*'

Mrs McDonald frowns, but it's a hopeful kind of frown, so I carry on, 'Animals don't understand the weather forecast, or satellite stations, or those, er, things that predict earthquakes—'

'Seismographs,' says Mrs McDonald, nodding as if to say – *Do go on*.

So I do. 'Animals can tell if there's going to be a big storm . . .'

Arf WOOF YIP YIP YIP agrees Way-Woof from next door.

Loudly. Her last yip ripped straight through my head like a chainsaw. This is a *nightmare*. I'm seriously worried now. Is Daisy in danger? I can

barely think straight; however, Mrs McDonald is waiting, so I continue as best I can.

'Er . . . before a big storm, sheep get their heads down and eat grass like there's no tomorrow . . .'

AARF ARRRF WOOF!

'. . . and gulls and seabirds head inland . . .'

YIP YIP HowwWWwwL!

'. . . and, er, and bees stay close to their hives . . .'

ARF.

'. . . and spiders completely abandon their cobwebs . . .'

AAARF YIP YIP.

Mrs McDonald smiles at me, but before she can say anything, Annabel (the pony) chips in.

'*We've* got a weather station on the south turret of Mishnish Castle, and *Daddy* says it's even more accurate than the Met Office.'

Oh, sigh. Annabel is always boasting about her house, her daddy and her pony. It's very boring. Mrs McDonald's smile vanishes as if she's wiped it off the whiteboard. Her voice goes all clipped and chilly and she says, '*Thank* you, Annabel. Now, back to animals forecasting the weather. How do they know? Do they remember bad storms in the past? Or are they

reading signs? What do you think the warning signs of a big storm might be?'

There's a lot of hands waving frantically in the air now, and Mrs McDonald is still talking, but I'm not really listening. It's suddenly gone quiet next door. I can't work out if this is a good thing or not. WayWoof sounded really upset. She sounded as if she was trying her hardest to warn us. Or even to warn someone *off*. To protect Daisy.

My stomach gives a little lurch. I hope Daisy's all right. After all, playgroup is her first venture out into the Big Wicked World on her lonesome. Without Mum. Daisy and I have been in the same classroom for the last few days since poor Miss McPhee vanished.* But now the little ones have a new teacher, so they've gone back to their room next door. That means I can't see what Miss Chin *does* in there with

---

* Before you ask, this was *nothing* to do with a Witch Baby spell.

them. For all *I* know, she could be teaching them Witchcraft. **Ha-ha**.

Actually, not so ha-ha. I wish I hadn't thought that. Now it occurs to me that WayWoof may well be silent because she's disappeared – perhaps Daisy's Up To No Good. Maybe she's turned her *entire class* into dragons. Or worse. What could be worse? Turning your class into slugs? Maybe *that's* why it's so quiet next door. Now I'm going to have to dream up

an excuse to go next door. Just to check; to make absolutely one hundred per cent sure that my baby sister is all right. I'm starting to put my hand up when I remember. Oh, **duhhhhh**.

Mum picks Daisy up at lunch time.

Daisy (and WayWoof) must have gone home. **Phew**. At least for the rest of today I won't have to worry about what on earth is going on next door.

But the little nagging doubt remains. What was wrong with WayWoof?

Eight:

Toad in a hole

The Toad was exhausted. She'd risen at five thirty, cooked breakfast (scrambled rat with shredded nettles), ironed the Chin's sober, grey teacher's skirt and spent *hours* persuading the tearful Nose that making money was easy. Under the Toad's guidance, the Nose was instructed to go to the dump and find some base metals for her first attempt at alchemy.[*] It was past midday when the Nose finally set off for the dump on foot, promising to return before supper. Waving goodbye to her sister with one warty flipper, the Toad could hardly wait to collapse on the sofa and enjoy some

---

[*] Sadly, this useful skill is no longer taught in schools. Alchemy is the study of how to turn base metals (tin, copper, lead, iron) into gold. These days, children only know reverse alchemy: how to turn gold *back* into base metals. It's not difficult. Here's how to do it: take gold, buy tin of fizzy drink, drink liquid - and there: one empty base metal tin. Gold into base metal in one easy step.

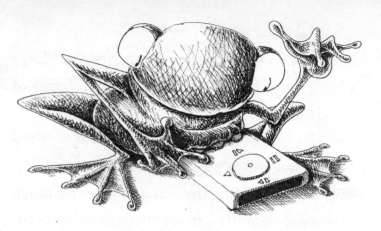

forbidden afternoon TV watching. She was squatting on the television's remote control, wondering which button to jump up and down on, when she heard the sound of a vehicle crunching across the drive outside, followed by footsteps and a knock at the front door.

Immediately the postman-cat and the playleader-sparrow began yelling for help, but since their pleas were in Cat and Sparrow, the Toad ignored them and hopped to the window to see who was outside. Peering out through the dusty glass, she could see a young man standing on the doorstep. At his feet was a large plastic crate full of what looked like boxes of chocolates.

'Oh, yesssss,' the Toad croaked. 'It's the Chin's computer shopping thingy!' And she leaped down from the window and bounded across the floor. *At last*, she thought delightedly. *Some real food for a change. No more rat ratatouille or nettle gumbo. Chocolate! Pizza!* She was just wondering what other delights might be in the young man's crate when she screeched to a stop at the front door.

What on *earth* did she think she was doing?

Heart hammering under her skin, the Toad clasped her head and gave a small moan. She was utterly horrified. To *think* she had been about to Open The Door. What a complete disaster *that* would have been.

You stupid, stupid, wart-encrusted, addle-pated slubberty-gubble, she thought. *You goggle-eyed, mush-brained tadpole. You quivering, useless blob of jellied—*

There was a determined **KNOCK, KNOCK** on the other side of the door, followed by a faint 'ER, HELLOOOOO?'

The Toad clasped her little webbed hands together as if in prayer. What to do? Oh, *what* to do? If she didn't answer, the young man might take his lovely crate away. The thought of missing all that wonderful food on the other side of the door gave her courage.

'Er, hellooooooo?' she quavered, in as pathetic a voice as she could manage. 'Young maaaan? I'm not feeling quite myself right now. Could you possibly just leave your delivery on my doorstep and I'll get it later when I feel better?'

There. Fear of discovery had practically dissolved the poor Toad into a little puddle of grease, sweat and tears, but she'd done it. Now, with any luck, the young man would do as he was told and go—

'Sorry to trouble you when you're feeling poorly, but I need a signature on this . . .' And to the Toad's dismay, a piece of paper and a pen came slipping and sliding *under* the door towards her.

Fortunately, before the dreadful day when the Toad turned herself into a toad,* she had always been the Sister of Hiss in charge of writing down spells and listing ingredients for potions. However, *that* was back when she had hands to write with. Now, with her warty, webbed little flippers, using a pen felt like trying to draw with a sharpened tree trunk.

However, the Toad had no choice, so, ignoring the background shrieks of: 'HELP HELP GET US OUT OF HERE HELP CALL THE POLICE!' in fluent Sparrow and Cat, the Toad signed the piece of paper and slid it and the pen back under the door.

Several very long and heart-hammering minutes later, she was rewarded by the sound of a vehicle driving away from Arkon House.

---

* Nope. That information is classified. The true story of how the Toad became a toad is written in invisible ink. The paper it is written on has been folded in three and tucked into a brown envelope, closed, licked and stuck down. Furthermore, the envelope has been tied up with string, sealed with sealing wax, wrapped in cling film, parcelled in baking foil, baked at 350°C for eight hours, cooled and then placed reverently in a metal shoebox under the Toad's bed. And There It Will Stay.

By the time we've had supper and I've done Daisy's nappy (**yeeeurghhh**), I'm ready for bed, even if Daisy isn't. WayWoof is curled up at the foot of Daisy's bed. She's not asleep, but then neither is Daisy. Daisy is waiting for me

to read her the next verse of *What Noise Does a Noisy Oyster Make?* Her face is bright pink from laughing so hard and she's staring at me, willing me to read her favourite page: the *What Noise Does a Squirty Squid Make?* page.* But

---

* I'm pretty sure you know that answer to this, but just in case you don't: a squirty squid goes, '*THHWRRRprrrTTTt-tPthhhhhTHWRRRRrppP.*'

I'm not going to do my dreadfully rude squirty squid impersonation. At least not until I find out what on earth was wrong with WayWoof today. After much thought, I decided that the best way to do this would be to get Daisy to make WayWoof speak in Human, and *that* way she could tell us *herself* exactly why she was barking at school.

I can hardly wait to hear what WayWoof sounds like. Will she have a Scottish accent? Will she have a deep growly voice? And how cool would it be to have our very own talking dog?

'O Beautiful Elder Sister of My Witchy Mistress,' I imagine her saying, 'your wish is my command. I only live to serve. Simply name that which your heart desires—'

And then I remember that if Daisy is doing a spell to make WayWoof talk, then she won't be able to keep the spell that makes WayWoof visible going as well.

One-Spell-At-A-Time, that's my little Witch Baby sister. So the only way to get to the bottom of WayWoof's Mystery Barking Fit is to *ask* Daisy to ask WayWoof. After all, Daisy magicked WayWoof into life, so she's probably the only person in the world who can understand what WayWoof is saying. The only problem is that Daisy's only a very little person. She can barely understand what *I'm* saying, let alone translate for her dog. But she's the only hope I've got, so here goes.

'Daisy? Could you help me? I need you to ask WayWoof something.'

'What noise squiddy squid make?'

'No-o-o-o. Not *right* now, Daisy. We'll do the squid stuff later, I promise. But now, could you ask WayWoof why she—?'

Uh-oh.

WayWoof is fading fast and Daisy's frowning so hard her face has practically folded in two.

'NOT ask WayWoof. Want squid. Wantit *now*. Lil go *tthhhprrr, chprrrt.*'

WHAT??? Oh *no*. Oh NO NO NO NOOOOOOO.

As Daisy makes her squirty squid sound, I find myself rapidly blowing up with air like a balloon. And just like a balloon, I drift slowly up to Daisy's bedroom ceiling, then bob helplessly in the corner above her door.

'Oh, come *on*, DAISY,' I try to say, but what

comes out of my mouth is a very loud
TH_WPRRRRRPR_RPH_{HH}H_PrrrCH_T.
Down below, Daisy shrieks with
laughter.

This isn't *fair*. Now Daisy's in control and I can't do anything about it. I don't like floating around, full of magical gas, feeling dangerously like I might go POP if I accidentally brush against something sharp. It's hot, stuffy, dusty and there are millions of cobwebs up here on the ceiling, and all of a sudden I've had enough.

'*DAISY*. Stop it. It's not funny any more. PUT me DOWN.'

Of course, all this does is make me go **Prrrt**, **frrrp**, **proot**, **pfff** all the more, and to make matters worse, every time I go **Prrt** or **Frrrp** or **Proot pfff**, I whoosh across the ceiling just like a deflating balloon. Fortunately Daisy is now laughing so hard she can't keep the spell going and, to my relief, I find that I'm slowly sinking back down to the floor, where WayWoof is fading back in.

Daisy shoots me a rather guilty smile as she

hands me her picture book, but I don't mind now. I still don't know what made WayWoof bark today, but I've worked out exactly how to find out.

'Hey, Daisy?' I say, opening her picture book and pretending to find a new page. 'Listen. Here's one we haven't had before. What noise does an invisible dog make?'

Daisy stops laughing as if somebody's turned her laugh switch to 'off'. She stares at me, and for some reason I shiver. **Woo hoo, I am Witch Baby**, her stare seems to say. Don't Mess With Me.

'A vizibble dog make a barky noise,' she says solemnly, then, just when I'd resigned myself to giving up my Get-WayWoof-Translated plan, she adds, 'A barky dog make a go-wayyyy-baaaad-lady noise.'

What? Before I can say anything, Daisy gives a huge yawn as if she wants to show me that she can handle anything WayWoof might bark at, even baaaad ladies, and dismisses me.

'Baba, Lil. Na-night. Tunna light off.'

Your wish is my command, **O Witch Baby**. I only live to serve.

Nine:

Ae fond kiss, Hiss

The front door of Arkon House opens and slams shut. In the kitchen, the Toad winces. **Uh-oh**, she thinks. *SOMEBODY'S had a bad day.*

The Toad has been planning a feast fit for a king. *Well*, she admits, *perhaps that is a bit of an exaggeration. Let's say it's a feast fit for a Hiss.*

She hears footsteps approaching and looks up in time to see the Chin totter across the living room and collapse onto a sofa.

'What a MORNING I've had. That was simply AWFUL,' she groans. 'The NOISE! My poor head. Horrible, horrible BEAST. That blooming dog. *Barking* incessantly. Couldn't even throw a crispy-tonsil spell to shut it up because it belongs to our precious Witch Baby . . .'

The Toad frowns, then remembers. Witch Baby's dog. Of course. Like Mary's Lamb, only invisible.

'And the SMELL. **Eughhhh**,' the Chin

continues, closing her eyes and slumping deeper into the sofa cushions. 'Horrible children too. With their soggy nappies and dribbly mouths – I tell you, I'm not sure if I can stand another' – the Chin yawns widely – 'another' – yawn – 'anoth—'

When the Toad pokes her head round the door, she finds her sister has fallen fast asleep in mid-rant. Perfect. Let her have a little afternoon nap. That way, the Toad reasons, she'll end up in a far better mood . . .

There's a pinging sound from the kitchen. Pizzas are nearly ready. Toad is just putting the finishing touches to supper when, for the second time that day, she hears the sound of a car engine outside. Could it be the Nose, back from the dump? No – it can't be. The Nose can't drive. Who can it be *this* time? In a panic, the Toad drops her spoon into the cauldron of chocolate sauce she'd intended for the pizza. The spoon bounces off the side of the cauldron and flips over, catapulting a vast gobbet of melted chocolate across the top of the cooker, most of which lands on the unfortunate Toad. Before she can react, the front door slams and all at once there are voices in the hall.

Voices?

In the living room, the Chin's eyes snap open and she's leaping off the sofa before she's even properly awake. Taking one wobbly step forward, she falls over the postman-cat and crashes to the floor with a howl of dismay.

There's a ghastly shriek from the direction of the kitchen, where the Toad has just discovered how hot her melted chocolate shower was. Coated in sauce and half hysterical, the Toad leaps into the living room just as the Nose

appears in the doorway, frantically signalling to her Sisters. To everyone's alarm, there is someone standing behind her.

Candles gutter and fizz in one of Arkon House's many draughts, but they cast a kindly light over the dining table where the Sisters of Hiss are entertaining their unexpected supper guest. Well, two of the Sisters, that is. In an earlier hissed conversation in the kitchen, the Nose and the Chin decided that their guest must

never discover that they are related to a talking Toad. Therefore, much to the Toad's disgust, she is shut in the kitchen and ordered to stay there until their visitor has gone.

Their unwelcome guest is their neighbour, Hare Harukashi. When the Sisters of Hiss first moved into Arkon House, it was Hare who gave them their computer. Because they'd lived on a mountain for the previous four hundred years, they had no idea how to use a mouse or a keyboard, so it was Hare who taught them. It was also Hare who told them about using the Internet to buy food. Hare is a very clever Japanese software designer. He is also a lonely widower, raising his daughter Yoshito all on his own. Poor Hare.

Lucky Hare too. He is blissfully unaware of how very fortunate he is not to have been turned into a cat, a sparrow or worse . . . How was he to know that a lift home from the dump was the last thing the Nose wanted? Hare saw what he thought was a damsel in distress there and stopped to offer assistance. The Nose had spent

a perfectly horrible afternoon sifting through rubbish, most of which was mouldy, maggotty and *not* made of base metal. When she finally gave up this pointless search, she was in a foul temper and all she wanted to do was go home and grind her teeth. Instead, she'd listened to Hare's chatter, fielded his questions and failed to get rid of him when he drove her home to Arkon House.

'Some more pizza, Mr Harukashi?' the Chin says through gritted teeth. For the millionth time she asks herself why on earth the Nose allowed this dreadful little man to give her a lift home? Why didn't she simply turn him into a woodlouse the first time he poked his nose into their lives? *So* much simpler. *So* easy to shut a woodlouse up. *So*—

'Delicious. I would love some, Miss Chin.' Mr Harukashi beams happily at her. 'Such a wonderful idea, chocolate pizza. What a marvellous, inventive cook you are.'

From behind the kitchen door they all hear

the unmistakable sound of something being smashed. Mr Harukashi's eyebrows practically disappear over the back of his head.

'Mice!' squeaks the Nose, then, realizing that not even a thousand mice could possibly have made such an unholy din, corrects herself: 'Silly me, I mean *rats*. Terrible problem we're having with rats. *So* noisy, *so* destructive, *so* . . .' And running out of things to say about their non-existent rat problem,* the Nose blushes, falls silent and wipes her nose on her napkin.

The Chin slides a slice of chocolate-coated pizza onto Mr Harukashi's plate. *Hurry up and go home*, she silently wills him, but Mr Harukashi is immune to her thought-waves. He praises the food, the candles, the comfort of the sofa, the warmth of the fire . . .

By the time Mr Harukashi buttons up his

---

* The Sisters of Hiss have no rat problem whatsoever. This is because since they moved in, every single rat that has set foot or whisker in Arkon House has been eaten.

coat and is finally standing on their doorstep, the Sisters of Hiss are completely flattened under the weight of all his praise. How on earth do humans cope with all this pleasantness?

But the worst is yet to come. As the Nose turns to go back inside, leaving the Chin to say the final goodbyes, Mr Harukashi stands on tiptoe and plants a smacking great kiss on the Chin's chin.*

* Luckily he can't quite reach her mouth. Had he been able to, she might have eaten him.

'Thank you, dear lady, for an evening I will never forget.' And bowing politely as he walks backwards down the drive towards his car, Mr Harukashi takes his leave.

Ten:

Spot on

Today starts badly. It's one of those horrible, wet, grey mornings when I wish I could just stay in bed. Our roof has sprung a leak, so Mum and Dad are busy running around with bowls and buckets to catch the drips. Someone forgot to order more milk, so nobly, Jack and I do without. This way Daisy can have the remaining milk for her breakfast. However, Daisy has again decided that breakfast cereal is really shampoo in disguise, and while Mum and Dad are distracted by the leaky roof, she starts remodelling her hair with handfuls of milky Toasty Oaties.

By the time we're finally ready to leave the house, we're all thoroughly fed up. Dad takes the car to drive Jack to school, and Mum, Daisy, WayWoof and I brave the rain. When at last we reach the school, we're drenched. Overnight, the playground has turned into a quagmire, so at morning break time we have to stay inside. This is a bit like being shut in with the wild animals in the zoo. The minute the bell rings, Vivaldi starts rifling through her rucksack. I watch. It's fascinating. She empties

it completely to find whatever it is she's looking for, so we all get to see what a pile of stuff she brings to school every day.

'Ewwww,' squeals Annabel. 'What is that disgusting-looking thing?'

'A giant tarantula leg,' mutters Vivaldi without looking up.

It's a hairbrush. Obviously. Even Annabel knew that. Annabel is probably going to go 'Ewwww' at everything in Vivaldi's rucksack, but she's fascinated, just the same. Even Craig and Shane have stopped swinging on their chairs and are showing some interest. They keep pushing and shoving each other and crashing into Donald, who is staring into the rucksack with his mouth open. Oh, boy. Feeding time at the zoo, I guess. Where would I be without Vivaldi?

As if she's heard my thoughts, Vivaldi looks

up and smiles at me, then shows us all her v-shaped prism for splitting light into rainbows.

'I've got hundreds of those,' Annabel mutters.

'*I've got thousands,*' squeals Shane, mimicking Annabel and adding nastily, '*Daddy bought them for meeeee.*'

'No you haven't,' says Annabel, her eyes flashing. 'Your parents couldn't afford thousands of anything.'

'Shut up, Annabel,' Jamie hisses, but before a big fight can erupt, Vivaldi pulls out a weird little bundle of matchsticks and string and holds it out for us to see. It's a tiny rope ladder.

'Ta-DAAAA,' she says. 'What do you think this is? C'mon, Annabel. Bet you've got hundreds of these too.'

But Annabel is too busy pulling faces at Jamie to pay any attention.

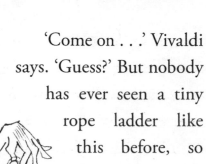

'Come on . . .' Vivaldi says. 'Guess?' But nobody has ever seen a tiny rope ladder like this before, so she explains. It's a spider ladder for hanging over the bath taps to allow spiders to climb out of the bath.

'Urrrrgh. Spiders. Ah hate them,' Shane moans, adding, 'Ah drown them.'

Poor spiders. But the spiders have Vivaldi on their side. Vivaldi, Spider-Saver. Poor Shane. She hunches her shoulders and bends over with her hands on either side of her face, and in a piercing whisper hisses, 'One day, Shane, you won't know where, and you won't know when, a giant spider will come along when you're in bed sleeping. And it will wrap you up in spider silk, then BITE you with its poisonous teeth – and then, when you're completely paralysed, it will begin to nibble you up, bit by bit—'

'Shut up,' says Shane, but he looks nervous, as if there might be a giant spider somewhere out there just waiting for—

'AAAAUUUGHHHHH, get it OFF MEEEE, YAAAAAAAAA!' he shrieks, flapping his arms round his head and leaping sideways. He runs around the classroom banging into desks and chairs, almost sobbing with terror.

Craig bursts into mocking laughter and yells, 'Calm doon, you fool. It was only me.'

'What a baby,' snorts Annabel, rolling her eyes. 'I don't mind spiders at all. We've got hundreds of them at home.'

126

Is there anything Annabel hasn't got already? Apart from a kind heart, that is.

Meanwhile Vivaldi pulls out a little woven bag full of tiny worry dolls. Yoshito goes into raptures over these, and without a moment's pause Vivaldi gives them to her.

'Not fair,' moans Annabel. 'I wanted them.' But Vivaldi ignores her completely because at last she's found what she was looking for.

Yum. It's her snack. Whatever it is, it looks and smells amazing. Vivaldi stuffs everything except the worry dolls and her snack back into her rucksack and everyone drifts away. Show over. My tummy gives a loud and envious **TWONGGG** as I follow Vivaldi across the classroom to our favourite seat on the radiator. All thoughts of snacks vanish though, because over on this side of the classroom we can hear WayWoof going nuts. In the room next door she is once again barking her head off.

'It must be because of Daisy's new teacher,' Vivaldi decides. 'There must be something about her that bugs WayWoof. The question is . . . *what*?' She raises her eyebrows, scratches her head and takes a bite of her snack.

'What question is what?' Jamie (the Gun) demands, adding, '**Ewwww**, what is that thing you're eating?'

'This?' Vivaldi pulls her mum's amazing home-made vanilla and walnut flapjack out of her mouth and examines it as if she'd only just found it stuck to the underside of her shoe. 'Oh – it's a Brussels sprout and spinach, gluten-free, organic' – Jamie backs away, but Vivaldi carries on – 'yak butter, goat's cheese and fermented soya bean paste tofu bar,' she finishes happily, adding wickedly, 'Want some?'

Jamie's pale face is answer enough, but he has been raised to be polite, no matter what. In a strangled voice he squeaks, 'Er. Gosh. No thanks. Awfully kind,' before turning and walking away very quickly.

'So' – Vivaldi smiles – 'that got rid of him. Now, shall we try and find out what's really going on next door with WayWoof?'

'But . . . we can't just barge into the nursery, can we?' I say.

'Yes we can,' Vivaldi says. 'You can pretend that your mum put Daisy's snack into your bag by mistake, and you've only just found it.'

This is a good plan, but Vivaldi doesn't know that I'm an absolutely hopeless liar. I'll turn bright pink and stammer if I have to tell a fib. Besides, I bleat, 'I've already eaten my snack, so I don't have anything to pretend with.'

'Here. Use mine,' and Vivaldi breaks off a square of her mum's amazing flapjack and hands it to me. I try not to drool too obviously, but it smells like heaven.

Watching from beside the mirror in the book corner, Annabel mimes being sick, but we both ignore her. Mrs McDonald pokes her head round the door and immediately Annabel grabs a book and pretends to be reading.

'Vivaldi and Lily,' Mrs McDonald says, 'off the radiator, dears. You'll boil your bottoms. I need you both to help me carry some things through next door for the little ones.' And she crooks her finger at us, as if to say, *Come on.* As

we join her in the corridor, she says, 'And Annabel, dear. Unless you've turned into a bat you'll never be able to read that book. You're holding it upside down.'

Closing the

classroom door, she gives us both a huge wink and sets off down the corridor; we follow along behind.

The Chin is also having a dreadful day.

Her chin has sprouted an enormous red spot, which is throbbing and pulsing as if at any moment it might launch into orbit around the Earth. And every time her chin throbs, the Chin is reminded of the previous night and the appalling behaviour of that dreadful little Harukashi man. *Kissing* her.

Eughhhhhh, it's a wonder she's only got one spot. After that kiss she feels she ought to be covered in millions of them. And now, to make matters worse, that horrible pesky dog is once again standing between her and Witch Baby, growling and baring its teeth every time the Chin moves so much as a wart's width in

her direction. Plus it's raining outside, pouring in fact, and first thing that morning Mrs McDonald decided that all the children would have to be kept inside at morning break.

'But . . . but what on earth am I supposed to do with them?' the Chin had asked.

Mrs McDonald peered at her over the top of her spectacles and sighed. 'I have no idea, Miss Chin,' she said wearily. 'That's your job as playleader. Perhaps you should play with them. Now, if you'll excuse me, I have to go and teach my lot.' And the Chin was left none the wiser.

Now, four minutes and twenty-two seconds into morning break, the nursery is on the brink of total meltdown. No sooner does the Chin try to sort out the woes of one group of weeping tots than another lot decide to inhale the sand in the sandpit, take a dip in the fish tank, eat the soil in the 'seeds we can grow' area or set the pet white mice free. The Chin leaps and spins from one disaster to another, and all the time that blasted dog is barking non-stop. Then, to her horror, she notices that her precious Witch Baby has removed all her clothes and is now running laps round the nursery stark naked, yelling, 'HahahahaHA! NOT catchit! Notta MEEEEE, the gin-jah-bud girl!'

Just as the Chin is about to make a grab for Witch Baby, the door opens and there, right in front of her, are those awful Blue Moon girls.

Since time began, witches have loathed Blue Moon children.

Blue Moon children can almost see.

Blue Moon children can tell if there's a witch nearby.

On their own, Blue Moon children are pretty powerless; after all, nobody pays any attention to a child who says, 'We've got a real witch teaching in our school.' But when you put two or more Blue Moon children together . . . **pffff**.

Then you've got trouble.

Then they back up each other's stories.

Then adults start to listen to what they're saying.

The Chin's heart rate speeds up and she begins to panic.

Lily is too aghast at the sight of Daisy running around in the nude to really pay any attention to the Chin. She bolts across the nursery in pursuit of her baby sister.

'**Hahahah**, Lillil. See Daisy run. NOT catch meee.'

'You're a toad, Daisy,' roars Lily. 'Come here NOW—' There's a crash as the sandpit topples sideways and falls to the floor.

Vivaldi isn't listening: she's too busy trying

to work out what it is about Miss Chin that seems All Wrong.

Behind her, Lily has managed to catch Daisy and is attempting to get her dressed again. 'Pants, Daze,' she mutters. 'Come on.'

'NO WANTIT!' yells Daisy. 'Want BUMBUMBUM.'

Vivaldi frowns, puzzling over the wrongness of Miss Chin. Could it be just because Miss Chin has such an enormous . . . spot on her . . . enormous chin?

Daisy breaks free of Lily and runs to WayWoof's side. Lily lets her. At least she's wearing her pants again. Even if they are on her head . . .

Vivaldi still doesn't

notice. She's staring at the Chin's chin. The spot is gruesomely fascinating. It's bright yolk-yellow in the middle with a rather dazzling pink rim and Vivaldi is fascinated. She's never seen a spot like that before . . .

The Chin is frozen with terror. *The child knows*, she thinks. *This awful Blue Moon girl knows what I am.*

Before she can stop herself, the Chin reacts. She does the first thing that comes to mind and hurls a Spell of Spots at Vivaldi. She hurls it so hard and so fast that Vivaldi feels as if she's being sprayed with grit.

'AAAAOOWWWWWWWw!' she roars, staggering backwards into the painting corner. There's a series of thuds as all the pots of paint topple over, tumble off the table and hit the floor, followed by the table and, finally, Vivaldi.

Result, thinks the Chin; then, rearranging her face into an expression of deep concern, she says, 'Oh! You poor, poor wee thing! Are you all right?' And she rushes forward to help Vivaldi to her feet, but really to check that her Spell of Spots has worked.

It has. Spectacularly.

Eleven:

A spot of bother

'Mum says you'd probably better not come round tonight,' Vivaldi says, her voice sounding muffled and far away.

She's on the phone in the kitchen of Four Winds, her house, and I'm on the phone in the hall of Station House, my house. Although we only live five minutes apart, now that Vivaldi's off school with the mystery spots, she may as well be on the moon.

141

'What did the doctor say?' I ask.

Vivaldi snorts. At least, I think that's what it is. Coming down the phone, it sounds like she's detonated a bomb.

'Ochhhh,' she groans, 'he poked my arm pits, listened to me breathe and stuck a thermometer under my tongue. He didn't say much at all.'

'So,' I say, dreading her answer, 'how long d'you have to stay off school?' What if she's off for a few days? A week? What will I do without her? I'll be on my own with the Wild Animals. **Aaaargh**. They'll eat me alive and spit out the bones. Craig will squash me flat. Shane will go through all the words he can think of that rhyme with my name until he gets to W. Annabel will sneer at everything I say, and Donald will just stare . . . and stare . . . and stare. And all the while there'll be a big black hole in the classroom where Vivaldi used to be. My friend, Vivaldi. My *only* friend, Vivaldi. I don't know anyone else at school. But maybe it'll be all right. Maybe she'll only be off school for a day. Or even two. I could last for two days. I hold my breath and cross my fingers for luck.

'That's the thing, Lil,' she sighs. 'The doctor didn't know. He said he'd never seen spots like mine before. He said I'm to stay off school for a week . . .'

A week? A whole week without Vivaldi? Oh, boy. This is going to be tough. No. This is going to be awful. All of a sudden I feel so lonely I want to cry. I can't do that, though. It's not me who's ill with the mystery spots. I stare bleakly at the wall. Vivaldi is still talking.

'. . . and he says I have to go for another check-up before I can come back to school. So . . . it might be longer than a week.'

Over a week? NO WAY. I feel ill. Suddenly I feel cold and shivery. It's the thought of having to go to school without Vivaldi. I don't think I can do it. My tummy gives a lurch, as if I'm about to be sick. Oh, NO. I wonder if Mum would allow me to stay at home if I tell her that just thinking about school makes me feel sick? Probably not. In fact, definitely not. No. There's no escape. I just have to hope nobody will notice how miserable I am. I also have to hope that when the Wild Animals are horrible to me, I don't burst into tears. If I do, I'll have to pretend I've got an eye infection. And a bad cold. But at least I'll be able to go and see Vivaldi after school. That'll help. A little bit.

'But worst of all is that no one is allowed to visit me in case I'm contagious.' Vivaldi sounds like she's about to burst into tears. I know exactly how she feels. What? I can't even go round to her house? How bad is that? Over a week without a single friend?

Poor Vivaldi. And yes, selfishly, poor me too. However, I remind myself, I'm not the one with spots, stuck at home, so I try to sound more cheerful than I feel.

'Don't worry – I'll phone you every night to let you know what you didn't miss.'

On the other end of the phone, Vivaldi sniffs. It sounds like a hailstorm, but I carry on, lying, 'And a week isn't that long, really.' *Yes it is*, I think. *A week is seven days times twenty-four hours times sixty minutes. A week is so long I can't even work out how many minutes I'll have to spend all on my own.*

There's a huge silence on the other end; then, in a tiny voice, Vivaldi whispers, 'But will you be all right?'

Me? I haven't got spots. I'm about to point

this out when she says, 'I mean, with that weird Miss Chin. What will you do?'

What with Vivaldi's spots and my future as the Friend-Free One at school, I'd completely forgotten about all that stuff.

'Hey,' I say, 'don't you worry about me. I'll be fine. After all, I've got Daisy to protect me, haven't I?'

There's a roar of laughter on the other end of the phone, and in a much-more-like-herself voice, Vivaldi says, 'Woo-hoo. Witch BAYBEEE. Don't mess with her.'

Too right. From where I'm standing in the hall, I can see Daisy. She's lying on the kitchen floor, laughing madly as WayWoof runs round in circles chasing her tail. Vivaldi's right. Miss Chin is a bit weird, but compared to my baby sister and her invisible dog, she's almost normal.

Next morning it's still raining. Our roof is leaking through a different hole and we've run out of things to take to school for a snack. After raking through the biscuit tin, Jack and I agree to divide an out-of-date energy bar between us. It looks pretty disgusting, but I'm sure I'll be able to persuade Daisy to do something about that. Dad and Jack take the car, and Mum, Daisy, WayWoof and I set off for school wearing wellies. We walk in single file along a little track, being dripped on by overhanging trees, and sometimes sploshing through really deep, muddy puddles.

Daisy loves the puddles – the deeper, the better. Back when we lived in Edinburgh, we'd walk through the middle of town to get to school, but up here in The Wilds, it's completely different. There are no traffic lights, no zebra crossings, no lollipop ladies and hardly any cars. Most of the other pupils live near enough to walk. However, just as we reach the start of the lane leading down to the school, a big black four-wheel drive **whOOshes** past us, throwing up a huge wave of mud, which narrowly misses soaking all three of us.* It skids to a stop a little way up the road and the back doors open to reveal The Gun and The Pony.

---

* I mean all four of us, but WayWoof is soaked already so a bit of extra mud probably wouldn't make that much difference.

No surprises there, but what is surprising is how utterly miserable Jamie and Annabel look.

They slam their doors shut in unison and the car reverses sharply, turns round and comes roaring back down the road towards us.

'Watch out!' Mum yells, but I'm already diving out of the way. The huge car races past, spraying muddy water in all directions. I check to make sure Daisy and Mum are all right and realize that WayWoof has gone.

Oh, dear.

There's a grinding sound, a **whoosh** and then complete silence from the far end of the road. I turn round slowly, dreading what I'm about to see. What has Daisy done now?

'Oh, brother,' Jamie mutters, his mouth open in dismay.

'Daddy – oh, your poor car!' Annabel squeaks, running past us to where her daddy's poor car has ground to a halt in the middle of an enormous puddle. The puddle is so vast, it could almost be a loch. It's also a brand new puddle because I know it wasn't there thirty seconds ago. This has to be one of Daisy's spells. There's no other explanation. Puddles this big don't just appear, no matter how hard it rains.

I stare at Daisy, but she's clapping her hands, obviously very pleased with herself.

'All WET now,' she crows. 'Road WET, sky WET, Lily WET, Mumma WET, bad car ALL WET . . .' And then, under her breath, 'Daisy NOT wet, hahahaha.'

I turn back to check what's happening with the car in time to see the driver's door fly open. A man with a red face jumps out, slips, loses his footing and – SPLOSHHHH – he's sitting in the puddle.

'Let's go,' Mum says in a rather choked voice. She is trying her hardest not to laugh. Her mouth twitches and her eyes shine. The red-faced man gets up and wades across the puddle, yelling loudly. Jamie is running towards him and Annabel is picking her way carefully round the edge with her head down. It's raining harder now, but even that doesn't mask the awful smell that suddenly fills the air.

'**Eughhhhh**,' Mum groans. 'That's dreadful. The drains must be backing up or something. **Ugh** . . .'

But the sudden stench is nothing to do with drains and everything to do with Daisy. Daisy and her invisible-but-smellable dog.

Spell's over. WayWoof's back.

Twelve:

Daylight robbery

For the third day in a row, the Nose is trying to make some money. Rather than go to the dump to find the raw materials to make gold or have another go at forging banknotes,[*] she's decided to go to the bank and steal some. So far, all she's done is wait in a long queue. Today, thanks to more advice from the Toad, she is wearing camouflage trousers, a hoodie and a pair of rose-tinted ski goggles. She is getting some very strange looks from other people in the queue, but she doesn't notice because she can hardly see. It took her over an hour and a half walking in the rain to reach the bank, and now, in the warmth, her goggles have steamed up so much it's like trying to see underwater.

---

[*] Not a success. Not only can the Nose not count, but she can't draw either. Even a short-sighted mole wearing bottle-bottom spectacles in a dark room would be able to tell that the Nose's forged banknotes were fakes.

As the Nose inches closer to the
counter, she is growing more and
more nervous.

This is her first attempt at a life of crime and already it's not going too well. She blinks and tries to focus, but she can't see. If only she hadn't worn these blasted goggles.

The queue edges forward. With each step closer to her goal, the Nose's heart beats faster and faster until she is convinced it's about to leap into her throat, pop out of her mouth and bounce across the floor, beating madly and alerting everybody to the real reason she is there.

'All RIGHT! Everybody on the FLOOR, NOW!'

The Nose jumps. *Hang on a minute,* she wants to say. *That's exactly what I was about to say.* All of a sudden there's an ugly man standing in the middle of the bank, waving a gun around and yelling at everyone.

Oh, Hiss, the Nose thinks. *Trust me to pick a bank that's already got its very own robber.* Hiss, spit and mutter. She's just wondering if she should leave and try to find another bank when the robber notices that she's still standing up.

'Right, missus,' a voice grates in her ear. 'Don't mess me about or I'll turn you into mince.'

The Nose is a bit confused by this, and turns round to peer blindly through her goggles at whoever is speaking. Something cold and hard is jabbed into her ribs, and a hand grabs her arm.

'Awwwright. Do it the hard way.

Everybody, face DOWN. Cover your eyes, or Big Nose here gets it.'

Big Nose? The Nose's blood pressure soars. Big Nose? How DARE this rude little robber refer to her like that? Despite the Chin's orders about spur-of-the-moment spells, the Nose is unable to stop herself. There's a shriek . . . then the bank robber's gun falls to the floor with a clatter. The gun lands on a cockroach* which didn't exist two seconds ago and squashes it flat.

Sensibly, the Nose decides that now is the right time to make herself scarce. Now, before any of the people obediently lying on the floor of the bank open their eyes and discover what really happened. Dragging the useless ski goggles onto her forehead, the Nose makes for the door and runs out

* This was a cockroach from the species *Yoosta robber banksii*. Rare, ugly and now extinct.

onto the street. Fortunately, because it's raining hard, there's no one around to see her, so she heads for home for the third day in a row, empty-handed.

It's morning break and I really miss Vivaldi. It's raining again, which means we have to spend the time stuck inside. I'm pretending to read one of Jack's music magazines, but it's hard going. I thought I'd look very cool and grown-up reading it, but I probably just look bored to death.

'Good Lord. What is that thing you're reading?'

Oh great. Jamie-the-gun. I'm not in the mood for dealing with him today. *Go away*, I will him silently, but it doesn't work.

'Ughhh. What band is that? They look like they never wash their hair. And they're so ugly.

D'you really like that kind of music? I would've thought you'd have been into bagpipe bands. You do play the bagpipes, don't you? That's why you drew the pipes on your name badge, isn't it?'

Shut up, Jamie, I silently beg him, but it's no use. On he goes, wiffling on about bagpipes, loud enough for everyone in our class to hear what he's saying. Craig and Shane smirk at each other. Oh, sigh. Thanks to Jamie, now the whole class knows that Lily MacRae (the New Girl With No Friends) plays the pipes. Great. Annabel is pulling faces as if she's just found out that I eat rats for breakfast and Donald's mouth has opened even wider.

Shane's laughing so hard his nose is running and Craig is grinning so I can see his fillings.

All of a sudden something inside me goes SNAP. I'm completely fed up with this. I hate this school. It's full of rude and stupid people and I wish I was anywhere but here. Nobody's ever going to be friends with me, and right now I don't care. I don't want to be friends with this lot. I don't care. I DON'T—

'Hey, Lily,' a soft voice says, 'do you want to share my snack?'

I spin round. It's Yoshito, and she's holding out a packet of prawn cocktail crisps. Wow. That's really, really nice of her, especially since she's normally so shy. It's really kind too. It's as if she sensed how cross and miserable I was feeling and tried to do something to help. I'm just about to reply when the big boys interrupt.

'**Pee-yeeew**,' says Shane. 'You don't want to eat any of her smelly crisps.'

'Nah,' adds Craig. 'Too right you don't, because I want them.' And he pushes his chair back and stands up.

Craig is enormous. He's almost as tall as Mrs McDonald and he makes Yoshito look like a shrimp. He leans over her and me and says, 'Come on. Hand them over.'

Now he's so close to us, I can see what he's drawn on his name badge, except I don't know what it is.* Whatever it is, it's hideous and there's a speech bubble beside it saying '**RRRRRRRRRR**'. Any second now, Craig looks like he'll go '**RRRRRRRRRR**', too.

Poor Yoshito. I can't just stand by and watch while Craig bullies her. I'm about

* I look it up later, though. It's a warthog, the animal least likely to win any beauty contests. Ugly and mean. A perfect fit for Craig.

to say something that will probably make sure Craig eats me after he's polished off Yoshito's crisps, when Shane steps in.

'Oi,' he yells. '*I* want her crisps.' And he stands up so fast, his chair falls over with a **crash**. His name badge flashes in the light. Shane the Shark. Shane the Squirt, more like. He may be the oldest in our class, but he's tiny.

Craig swings round to face Shane, and for a moment I think Shane might be in real trouble . . . when the door opens and Mrs McDonald comes in.

'BOYS!' she roars. 'I need some muscle to help me carry in the hot lunches. Craig, Shane and Jamie. Stir your stumps, lads, and come and give me a hand.'

It's every bit as magical as one of Daisy's spells. Mrs McDonald must have worked her Hairy Eyeball trick again. Craig and Shane are transformed from dangerous, hulking, crisp-stealing bullies into helpful boys who meekly follow Jamie out of the classroom. Yoshito and I are left to share her crisps, but it's really hard work talking to someone who's so shy. I know I'm being totally ungrateful, but I'd rather be

on my own. I'm almost as shy as she is, and by the time morning break is over we've run out of things to say.

Pets? Yoshito's dad keeps koi carp in an ornamental pond in their garden.

Favourite food? Fish fingers.

Favourite story? *The Little Mermaid*.

Favourite film? *Finding Nemo*.

I'm beginning to understand why she drew a fish on her name badge. Yoshito is really sweet, but she's not Vivaldi. I feel lonelier than ever.

We have art in the afternoon and I ask Mrs McDonald if I can make a get-well-soon card for Vivaldi. Mrs McDonald thinks this is such a good idea, she suggests that everyone in the class makes one. Craig and Shane pull hideous faces, but eventually they settle down and draw monsters covered in oozing spots. *Ah*, I think. *Self-portraits*, then I immediately wish Vivaldi was sitting next to me to share my feeble joke. However, if she was sitting next to me, we wouldn't be spending the afternoon making get-well cards, which is actually rather good fun. The little ones in our class love anything that involves paint, glitter and glue, so they make card after soggy card for Vivaldi. Yoshito draws a beautiful fish with spots, Annabel sighs and looks out of the window, and Jamie draws a pretty feeble stick-man, tears it up, draws another, tears that up too, then spends the rest of the afternoon staring at his fingernails.

When everyone has finished, Mrs McDonald gathers up all the cards and gives them to Vivaldi's little sister

Mozart to deliver. I wish I could deliver the cards myself, but I'm still not allowed anywhere near Vivaldi in case she's infectious. We're all waiting to see if Mozart breaks out in a rash of spots, but so far she hasn't. I've got my fingers crossed that this means that Vivaldi isn't infectious and will be able to come back to school really soon. My card is a drawing of WayWoof standing outside Vivaldi's house, with a speech bubble coming out of her mouth that says:

```
AWOOO!
I really miss
YOUUUUUU!
```

And just in case Vivaldi thinks this is too soppy for words, I draw a cloud hanging over WayWoof's tail, and inside it I write:

PEE-YEWWWWW!
Was that
YOU?

I hope she likes our get-well cards and I hope she gets well soon. And last but not least, I hope it stops raining.

Thirteen:

Brewing up a storm

It's only the end of her third day at nursery, but the Chin is barely able to drag herself home. She is completely pooped. Looking after small humans is a lot harder than she expected. Looking after small witches is even worse. Much as the Chin hates to admit it, precious, wonderful Witch Baby is turning out to be a complete monster. The Chin shudders. Her skirt is streaked with paint, her blouse is torn and her long white hair has come undone.

For two pins, she thinks, *I'd let Witch Baby grow up as a normal human.*

Every time she turned her back on Witch Baby, the tot would cast a spell. First of all she turned all the books in the book boxes into birds. The birds flew around the room raining poo from the ceiling, which made all the other children shriek like banshees. And no sooner had the Chin turned the birds back into books than Witch Baby started blowing pink bubbles.

Thousands of bubbles began floating around the nursery, sticking to everyone and everything before exploding in a hail of sherbet. Finally, to add insult to injury, Witch Baby sneaked up behind the Chin, clapped her tiny hands, and before the older witch could do anything to cancel the spell, she found herself floating up into the air.

Remembering this, the Chin has to stop on her way home and take several deep breaths to calm herself down.

When did Witch Baby become so powerful? she wonders. And what, if anything, can the Sisters of Hiss do about it? These questions remain unanswered when the Chin arrives home. To her annoyance, she finds that supper is not ready, and for the third day in a row the Nose hasn't managed to make any money at all.

'Again?' The Chin cannot believe her ears. 'You're kidding. Tell me that you haven't failed *again*!'

'Failed?' the Nose squawks. 'What is this? An exam in Making Money? YES. I failed to make money. NO. I do not wish to try again. Frankly I'd rather eat raw rat.'

'That's tomorrow's supper,' mutters the Toad, slicing a pizza into cubes and realizing too late that the little bluey-green speckles are mould, not Italian seasoning.

'Supper?' says the Chin. 'Now you mention it, where is my supper?'

'Supper is off,' says the Toad, tipping the mouldy pizza into the bin and adding insincerely, 'Sorry.'

Smoke begins to trickle out of the Chin's ears. This is not what she hoped to hear. There has to be something to eat, surely? What has

the Toad been doing all day? The Chin is so tired and hungry that she feels like throwing a tantrum. She learned how to do this at nursery today. Tantrums are what human children throw when things don't go Their Way. Human children scream blue murder, hold their breath till they turn purple, then fling themselves down and drum their heels on the floor. However, the Chin doesn't have the energy to throw a tantrum right now. Looking after Witch Baby and her classmates is more than enough for one day.

'I'm starving,' she says. 'I don't care if supper is off, on or sideways. Just put something on a plate and get a move on. Some of us have been working today . . .'

At this, the Toad quivers and tiny flecks of foam appear at the corners of her mouth.

'I would have made supper,' she says, 'but there's no more food left. Someone was supposed to be making money to buy some food, but someone failed to make so much as a single penny.'

The Nose turns purple. Steam whistles out of her ears like a boiling kettle. Her heels begin to drum on the floor. 'Are you talking to me?' she says, in a menacingly soft voice.

'Yes,' says the Toad, thrusting her chin in the air. 'And? What if I am? What're you going to do about it?'

'Er, um, hang on, Sisters? Dear Sisters? Shall we talk about this . . . ?' says the Chin, sensing too late that there's about to be a fight.

The Chin is right. There's about to be a huge fight. **Woo, hoo**. Here it comes. Head for the hills. RUN! HIDE! A **Witch Fight** is like thunder and lightning but a squillion times more frightening.

The Nose turns bright red and sparks shoot out of her nostrils.

She hurls a stream of oaths and curses at the Toad, then spins round and flings a few more in the Chin's direction. Immediately the Toad and the Chin erupt with rage; one in a torrent of green lava, the other in a blazing tower of flame. RUN! HIDE! Don't stop to pack. Just GET OUT OF RANGE! When the Sisters of Hiss fight, their rage spills across the neighbourhood

like ink spilled across a
page. Already their fury
has caused a vast
thunderstorm to build
in the skies above
Arkon House. Fingers
of lightning flicker

along the horizon, heavy spells rumble and crash in the distance and the ground trembles in sympathy.

BANG CRASH!! RRRRRRRRRRRUMBLE . . . FLASH!

Then, as quickly as it began, it's over.

The Sisters of Hiss pick themselves up, dust themselves down and peer around at the damage they've done. In their RAGE, they have made a terrible mess. Their living room is trashed. Bits of the sofa are embedded in the ceiling, bits of the ceiling are scattered across the dining table, and apart from the computer, the only things that appear to have survived are the cat and the sparrow. One of these is cowering in a corner;

the other is clinging
to the curtain rail.

Outside, lightning
flashes and thunder rolls
deafeningly across the
horizon from east to west.
A year's worth of rain
will fall in the space of the
next few hours. Weather
forecasters will scratch their
heads in puzzlement. Where
could this bad weather have
come from? Only the Sisters
of Hiss know, and they're not
telling. Despite their promises

about not using magic, the Sisters are extremely proud of the raw power they can command. As the Chin remarks later that evening, 'This storm is proof that we, the Sisters of Hiss, are still the bees' toenails, the cats' knees and the sparrows' pyjamas.'

No sooner has this boast left her lips than there's a HUGE flash of lightning and the lights go out.

Fourteen:

Big weather

I am fed up. I don't think I've ever felt quite so bored or lonely. This is even worse than when we moved here from Edinburgh, although that wasn't a whole lot of fun either. But school without Vivaldi is the pits. Even Daisy's got more friends than me. Tonight she's going to the little snakes-as-laces boy's house for tea. She's been invited to two parties at the weekend and she keeps on taking the party invitations off the fridge and cooing at them. Although I'm really happy that everyone likes Daisy, I'm beginning to feel like some sort of sad Lily-No-Friends. Watching my little sister getting ready to go out reminds me that I have nowhere to go. Sniff.

Jack's babysitting until Mum comes back after driving Daisy the Party Animal to her dinner date. Unfortunately, his idea of babysitting involves turning on the TV, sticking his earbuds in both ears – Tss tsss – and slinging one of Mum's frozen tubs of lasagne into the microwave to heat up for supper.

Tss, Tss.

Boring.

I'm upstairs practising my pipes. Out of consideration for Jack's eardrums, I'm only using my chanter (the wee mouthpiece thingy) without the bag and drones attached. That way, Jack won't bleed from both ears when I start playing. Plus there'll still be glass left in the windows of our house when Mum comes back.

I should be practising with the full set – chanter, drones and bag. To do that, I'd have to go down to the other end of our garden; the noise I make up here in my bedroom is so loud, I would blow the windows out. I'm not kidding. The bagpipes are LOUD. When I play

them outdoors, I'm pretty sure they can hear me in the Outer Hebrides, if not in Norway. All the birds for miles around fall out of the trees and lie sobbing on the ground. Crops wilt, fruit withers and insects explode in mid-air. However, that isn't going to happen tonight because it's pouring with rain and I heard a rumble of thunder just a minute ago. There's

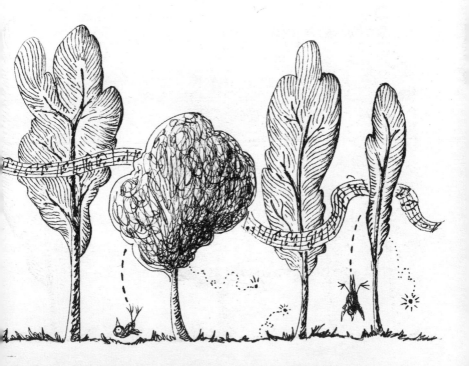

no way I'm going outside to play my pipes now. Imagine – there I'd be, in full swing, going, *Waily, waily Dweeeeeee, waily, waily, Dweeee, Pweeeeee*, and then, **FLASH**, frizzle, frizzle, *Dweeeeeeeeeee*.

No thanks. I choose life. I'll play inside tonight, even if it's not as much fun. Although I'm embarrassed to admit I play the pipes, I really LOVE them. I LOVE making such an enormous sound. Tonight it's a concert for bagpipes and thunder.

CrAsH! **RrrumBLE**! *Waily waily waily dweeeeeeeeeee*!

As I play, I think about Daisy. I'm hoping she doesn't cast any spells while she's away from home – or is this thunderstorm a little something that Daisy has magicked up to impress her friend? I can hardly bear to think what might happen if it is. Imagine – the little

boy will show Daisy his collection of soft toys: his furry lion, his pink penguin, his dangly monkey, his . . .

Daisy will smile sweetly, WayWoof will begin to fade and then the fun will begin. She will show the little boy how she can bring all his toys to life. Before her new friend can blink, his bedroom will be knee-deep in lion poo and there'll be penguins diving into the bath and monkeys swinging from the curtain poles.

CrAsH, FLASH! goes the storm outside. Oh, please, don't let it be Daisy making it do that! I try my hardest to put all my worries about Witch Baby to one side and concentrate on playing, but it's not easy. Every time I inhale, I can smell something burning. I stop playing and sniff. And sniff again. There's definitely something burning. I drop the chanter and run to open my bedroom door.

Sniff. Uh-oh.

The smell is a lot stronger now – it's coming

from downstairs. It's horrible, like burning plastic.

'JACK?' I yell, suddenly frightened. 'JAAAACK?'

Just as it dawns on me that he won't be able to hear me because he'll have his earbuds in, I see him sprinting down the hall yelling, 'AaAAAAAAAAAAAAAAAArgh.'

We both arrive in the kitchen at the same time, coughing and gagging because the smell

has become a thousand times worse. The kitchen is full of dirty-looking smoke and Jack is flapping his hands at me, although I can't tell if it's to tell me to stand back or to clear the air. He hauls open the back door, and immediately cold, fresh air pours into the kitchen. Then Jack stuffs his hands into Mum's oven mitts, opens the oven door – and a huge coil of black smoke unwinds into the kitchen.

Aha, I think. *Dinner is served.* Yum.

Poor dinner. Poor Jack, too. But honestly. What a complete twit he is. Even I know better than to put a plastic tub of lasagne into a hot oven. A microwave, yes, but in a normal oven, plastic melts. Boy, does it melt. **Eughhhhhh**.

Jack removes the whole metal oven shelf, which now has the blackened remains of our supper welded to its rungs. He runs with it, smoking hideously (the shelf, not Jack), into

the back garden.
Great. Dinner and
a show.

'Blasted STUPID
thing!' he roars,
hurling the oven shelf
onto the path. It turns
a cartwheel, bounces
a couple of times and
lands in a puddle, hissing
like an annoyed snake.

The kitchen stinks of
burned plastic, so Jack leaves

the door open to the rain. Outside, the world looks as if it's dissolving. Flashes of lightning light up Jack's pale face and I can see that he's not having the best of days. For once, his earbuds are dangling from the neck of his T-shirt rather than stuck in his ears.

'Mum's going to kill me,' he groans. 'What a stupid thing to do. For heaven's sake, how dumb am I?'

I could answer that, but Jack looks so miserable that I decide it wouldn't be fair to say anything to make him feel any worse. So instead I say, 'Let's see if there's something else we can eat,' and we head for the fridge.

Hmm. Jack peers over my shoulder. Oh dear. There's a yellowish cabbage, some tired broccoli and a bowl of squishy-looking tomatoes. Tucked in behind where the milk should be, if only someone would remember to buy some, we find a shrivelled chilli and a furry lump of green mould. **Aaargh**. The fridge is bare. What are we supposed to eat? Then I remember that Mum was going to go shopping while Daisy was at her friend's house. That means it will be hours before they come home.

Meanwhile Jack has given up on the fridge and is now rooting through the kitchen cupboards. The kitchen is freezing cold, rain is pouring in the open back door, but there's my brother, on a mission to find something to eat. With a whoop of triumph he pulls a tin out of a cupboard and waves it triumphantly round his head.

'BEANS!' he yells. 'Beautiful beans. Beans, beans, the protein of choice, the more that you eat, the louder the noise . . .'

Oh dear.

'Beans, beans, the wonderful fruit,' he continues. 'The more you consume . . .'

'The louder you PROOT,' we chorus.

Then there's an enormous clap of thunder and the lights go out.

'Jack?'

'Lil?'

It's pitch black. We find a torch, then stumble around trying to find batteries that aren't totally flat. After what feels like hours, Jack remembers our old camping gas lantern

and we grope about in the darkness for matches
to light it with.

Much later, when Mum and Daisy finally
return home, they find Jack and me sharing
the tin of beans. Cold beans. Jack has dolloped

mayonnaise on top of his, and in the pale gaslight this looks even worse than it sounds.

Daisy has had a wonderful time at little snakes-as-laces' house. She calls her new friend Dugger, which probably isn't his real name, but Jack makes Daisy fall about laughing when he says, 'Hey, kid, how's Duggaduggadugga doing?'

At Dugger's, Daisy has been watching TV, drinking fizzy juice and eating pizza. Mum rolls her eyes as she tells us this, because she thinks that TV rots our brains in exactly the same way as fizzy drinks rot our teeth. But as she says, it's making friends that's important, and Daisy seems to have managed that, despite being a Witch Baby.

Tonight Daisy doesn't look like a little witch. She looks completely normal. She jumps when there's a loud thunderclap, and buries her head in Mum's cardigan when the lightning flashes. The storm is still crashing and flashing outside, but I'm pretty sure it has nothing to do with Daisy because right in the middle of a deafening crash, WayWoof sticks her paws up on the table, stretches out, and with one large slurp, neatly removes all the mayonnaise from Jack's beans.

Yeeeurch.

'Ooohhh, bah dog,' Daisy says, leaning against my legs and gazing up at my face. 'What noise make a bah dog, Lil?'

Oh, I think we all know the answer to that one.

A bah dog makes a **Prrrffffft** noise.

Gag. **Cough**. *No, Mum, it wasn't me.*

Fifteen:

Beastly relations

Just for a change, it isn't raining when I wake up. I get dressed slowly, but no matter how much I yawn and stretch, I can't seem to wake up. Brushing my teeth, I stare in the mirror, wondering if I've caught whatever it is that Vivaldi's got, but I don't look any different from how I looked yesterday.

Daisy's already eating when I go downstairs. Just like yesterday, she's rubbing breakfast in her hair. Oh, groan. Already, today looks like it's going to be exactly the same as yesterday. Which means . . .

. . . suddenly I feel awful. Today will be another day with no Vivaldi. Another day pretending that I'm fine – *No, really, I'm perfectly happy on my own*. Or even another day trying to dredge up fishy things to discuss with Yoshito. I stare at my cornflakes, wondering how much longer I have to wait until Vivaldi is better.

Across the table from me, Jack is hoovering down a vast trough of porridge. He's making the most disgusting, slurping, sucking sounds as he shovels the horrible grey mush into his mouth. I don't like porridge and neither does Jack, but he has rugby practice today, and he always has porridge because he says it gives him the energy of ten mid-fielders. **Sluppa**, splott, he goes. Schlooop. I try to tune him out, but no matter how hard I try, porridge sounds are all I can hear. As if today wasn't bad enough, I now find I'm related to a beast.

'What a complete pig,' I mutter under my breath, too quietly for Jack to hear, but not, alas, Daisy. I always forget that Daisy has ears like satellite dishes. Her mouth falls open.

'Notta pig,' she says, but because her mouth is full of partly chewed toast, she doesn't so much say this as spray it.

Lovely. I'm surrounded by beasts. Jack's still going splutt, **sluppa**, and now Daisy's spraying everything around her in toast-mush.

'You're both pigs,' I hiss, pulling the cereal packets across the table to form a barrier

between me and my relatives. I'm completely fed up now. Fed up to the back teeth with my brother, my sister, my school . . . I close my eyes and push the heels of my hands into my eye-sockets. Blackness rises up in front of me.

'Notta pig,' Daisy insists in the background.

Sluppa, Sploot, **schlepp**, goes Jack, but the noises he's making sound different now. Louder and clearer, as if he's closer to me. Huh?

I open my eyes. Nope. He's no closer. I can't see him properly though. He's reading the paper, and every so often his arm comes round the front page and lifts a spoonful of porridge up to—

Hang on.

That's not a hand snaking round the paper.

No way. NO WAY. Daisy? 'Daze? DAZE? What are you playing at?'

'Notta pig, Lil. Dack's an effalunt. Hahahahaha.'

Oh, help. She's right. The bits of Jack that I can see have gone all grey and wrinkly. As I gape at him, a snaky grey trunk whips round the paper, whiffles about on the tabletop, finds the rim of the porridge bowl, dips into it and . . .

SNOOORK.

It's such a funny sound that I choke on my cornflakes. Daisy is staring at me, her mouth a round O of delight.

SNURRRK-A-SNORRRK.

'What noise a hungry Dack makes?' she whispers, and I'm just about to reply when a clot of porridge gets stuck in Jack's trunk and he reverse-snorts it out across the table.

THHHHWORRRKSLUPP. It bounces off the tabletop – **SPWOTTT** – and hurls itself straight into the rubbish bin with such force that the bin rocks from side to side, going *Duggaduggaduggaduggadugga.*

Daisy bursts into peals of laughter. Spell over. WayWoof reappears under the kitchen table and Jack peers round the paper. He has a normal nose, I'm glad to report.

'What time is it?' he asks, obviously unaware that two seconds ago he was drinking porridge through his trunk. Poor Jack. He hasn't a clue.

Time to go. We have the usual five minutes of MacRae madness as we sort out lunch money, snack, shoes, gym kit, bags and homework. Dad's away on business today so Mum's driving Jack to school. Daisy and I sit in the back of the car and watch the world go by. Daisy gives a running commentary on what's going on outside the window, but I'm not really listening because I'm sinking back into going-to-school gloom.

'TreetreetreehousemooooCow, tacktoetreetreetree . . .'

Even my baby sister has more friends than I do. I wish Vivaldi would hurry up and get better.

'Carcarlorryttacktoe,sopssops sopstreetree.'

My breath is misting up the car window and I stab at it with my finger, making little marks in the mist which fill up and start to run down the glass. The car slows down and stops. Jack undoes his seat belt, leaps away from Mum (in case she tries to kiss him) and climbs out, calling goodbye over his shoulder. I watch glumly as a group of his friends run across to greet him. Maybe if I learned to play rugby, I'd have loads of friends like Jack. He's really good at sports, but I'm rubbish. I can barely swim, I duck if anyone throws a ball at me and I hate gym. I can run really fast, but that doesn't seem to help me make friends. As Mum drives away, I can see Jack surrounded by schoolmates, all obviously delighted to see him. I try to imagine Jamie and Annabel being delighted to see me.

'Jolly good show,' Jamie would say, shaking my hand politely. 'Gosh. We've been ever so

frightfully bored waiting for you to show up.'

'So glad you could make it,' Annabel would breathe, leaning in to kiss me on both cheeks.

Urrrgh, keep away, I'd think, *with that awful stinky seal breath*, but it's too late . . .

MwAH, MwAH, kiss, kiss, she'd go and—

Ughhhh. NO. I can't do it. No matter how hard I try, I can't do it. I simply can't imagine being friends with them. What about the rest of my class? What about Craig?

Craig would slap me on the back and roar, 'How's it gawn, Lily, eh?' and then accidentally knock me unconscious with a football.

Shane? Yoshito? Donald? Mozart? They're all OK, but the problem is that none of them is Vivaldi. I happen to like Vivaldi best. *Never mind*, I tell myself. *She'll be back soon.*

'Treetreegrasstacktoe,seepseep baaabaaabackseep.'

As we drive away from Jack's school and head for Daisy's and mine, it starts to rain. Big fat drops batter the car's roof and the fields on either side of the road look like they're dissolving. Mum groans and switches on the windscreen wipers.

'Disgusting weather,' she remarks, to no one in particular.

''Gusting,' Daisy agrees. At her feet, WayWoof sighs in sympathy.

'Honestly. Ever since we moved here, the weather's been filthy,' Mum sighs. 'I'm sick of the endless rain. So depressing.'

''Pessing,' Daisy says. 'So, so, so 'pessing.'

Mum smiles at Daisy. 'What we need,' she says, 'is some interesting weather. I wish it would do something exciting like snow.'

'Snow?' I squeak. 'In September?'

Even Daisy is aghast. 'SNOW?' she echoes. 'Intemba? No, no, no SNOW.'

'Yes, snow,' says Mum. 'I remember one year, long before any of you were born—'

'I borned too,' Daisy interrupts and Mum laughs.

'No, Daze,' she teases. 'We found you at the bottom of the garden under a daisy bush.'

Then she parks the car, switches off the engine and turns to look at me properly. 'I know you're feeling a wee bit lonely, Lil. It's hard work making new friends. All I can say is: give it time. You're such a great person – thoughtful, funny, kind, slightly mad . . .'

Thanks, Mum. You can stop now.

'. . . helpful, clever, snarky, brave. Once people get to know you, they'll be queuing up to be friends with you. Just you wait. Till then, if it's any help, we all love you to bits and think you're brilliant.'

'Bill yint,' Daisy agrees, then, 'No SNOW?'

And we all burst out laughing. We sit in the car for a bit longer, till all the windows steam up. Then the bell goes and Daisy and I head inside.

Sixteen:

The Hisses swap

'Won't anyone notice that you're not me?' the Chin asks. She's standing outside the bathroom, talking to the Nose through the door.

'No,' the Nose sighs, gazing at her reflection in the broken mirror* over the sink. 'Today, even Mummy wouldn't be able to tell us apart.' And to prove her point, she throws open the door.

The Chin gasps. There, standing in front of her, is the Nose. But now the Nose looks just like the Chin. Exactly like.

* Every mirror in Arkon House is broken. Each time the Sisters of Hiss look in a mirror, they break it. This is probably not because they're beautiful.

'It's just a teeny, weeny little spell,' the Nose mutters. 'I know we said no more magic but I can't very well turn up at Witch Baby's school pretending to be you if I look like me, can I?'

The Chin frowns. The Nose is right, but a promise is a prom—

'AND,' the Nose continues, 'let's not forget that swapping jobs was your idea. You're the one who said making money was easy-peasy, so . . . let's see how easy you find it. Ready?'

'Absolutely,' the Chin says, lying through her teeth.

And off they go, in the rain. Unlike the magical downpourings of the night before, this rain is the ordinary, north-western Scottish kind of rain: cold, wet and unwelcome.

The Chin is heading for the nearest library to borrow a book about how to make money. She is feeling nervous, and is highly likely to cast a spell turning everyone in the library into worms, slugs or even warthogs if she thinks she's in any danger of being unmasked as a witch.

Uh-oh. **NIGHTMARE.**

The Nose is heading for Lily and Daisy's school. Unlike the Chin, the Nose will have no hesitation in eliminating everyone within a ten-mile radius if she thinks Witch Baby is becoming too human.

Uh-oh. **DANGER.**

Behind them, the Toad blows kisses, then shuts the front door and heaves a sigh of relief. Now she has the house to herself. She sets a pan of nettles and dandelions to

simmer on the cooker and goes through to the living room to begin tidying up the mess left after their fight. Outside, the rain keeps on falling.

'I'll let you do your own milk and sugar, dear,' Mrs McDonald says, passing a steaming mug of coffee across to the Nose. It's morning break time, and both teachers are holed up in the staffroom. 'I couldn't keep them in again,' Mrs McDonald continues. 'I know it's tipping down outside, but if the children had been cooped up for another day, they'd have started sprouting roots. Children need to get outside and run around, don't you think?'

'Mmmmn,' the Nose murmurs, but she's not really listening. She's wondering what on earth she's supposed to do with the cup that Mrs McDonald has handed her. It's full of a black and steaming potion that smells terrible. Can it be that Mrs McDonald is trying to poison her? Surely not. No. Mrs McDonald has poured hot water into another cup of identically horrible liquid and is taking tiny sips from it. That rules out poison. The Nose peers into her cup. **Eughhhh**.

'You'll have to go out and supervise them, though,' Mrs McDonald says, staring through the staffroom window at the children running around outside. Suddenly she leaps forward and raps on the window with her knuckles. 'NO! Craig. Not by the neck, dear. He'll choke.' Then, without a pause for breath, she turns back to the Nose and continues, 'Can't leave the wee mites from the nursery running around in the rain on their own. Before we know it, they'll be up to their armpits in mud.'

The Nose tries to look interested, but really

she couldn't care less. The only child she's concerned about is Witch Baby, and right now she's very concerned indeed. She has just seen her holding hands with another child. Holding hands? Real witches would rather eat wasps than hold hands. Holding hands is what humans do, and is therefore most definitely *not* how a witch is supposed to behave. The Nose vows that if she finds any more evidence that Witch

Baby is turning human, then she's going to grab her and cast a Vortex of Vanishment spell across the whole of the Highlands of Scotland. When she's finished doing that, there won't be so much as a midge left to tell the tale—

Suddenly the Nose is aware that Mrs McDonald is staring at her.

'Drink up, dear,' the teacher says, 'then get your coat. I can lend you an umbrella if you need one.'

The Nose realizes that Mrs McDonald has no intention of joining her in the rain. Mrs McDonald intends to remain in the staffroom, staying warm and dry, reading brightly coloured magazines, while the Nose gets cold and wet. It dawns on the Nose that working with small children and their teachers might be tougher than she thought. Stifling a strong desire to turn Mrs McDonald into a cockroach, she downs her coffee in three scalding gulps and heads out into the rain.

The Chin is also having a perfectly horrible morning. To her disgust, her best pair of black pointy-toed boots have sprung a leak, causing her to wince every time she goes through a puddle. Cars whoosh past, spraying her with water, and she's so wet and miserable she nearly walks straight past the library. She skids to a stop, turns and almost screams out loud. There, on the pavement in front of her, is a sign advertising the latest newspaper headline. Unlike the Nose, who cannot read, the Chin understands exactly what the sign says:

POLICE STEP UP SEARCH FOR MISSING POSTMAN AND TEACHER

The Chin sways and the world around her spins slightly. For a moment it's as if the newspaper headline is pointing an accusing finger straight at her. After all, she knows exactly where the missing postman and teacher

are, right now. They're both in Arkon House.
One is fast asleep with his little furry paws in
the ashes of the hearth and the other is dozing

on a poo-speckled perch with her head tucked under her wing. Both of them are very much alive, despite being the victims of the Sisters of Hiss's wickedness. If the postman and the teacher could speak, the Sisters of Hiss would be in trouble. BIG trouble.

The Chin has a sneaking suspicion that kidnapping two people is probably a Very Bad Thing. This will be why the police are involved in the search. The Chin begins to shake like a jelly. What if the police find a clue that leads them to Arkon House? From her many hours watching daytime TV, the Chin knows that the police always get their man. Or woman. Or, in this case, witch.

Another, far more terrible thought occurs to the Chin and she can hardly stifle a squeak of dismay. What if the police are already on their way to Arkon House? Abandoning all thoughts of the library, the Chin picks up her skirts and begins to sprint for home, hoping against hope that she's not too late to avert disaster.

Seventeen:

The spelling test

At break time we're all sent outside in the rain. I can't believe Mrs McDonald thinks this is good for us. It's pouring. We're going to get drenched. The littlies in Daisy's class think this is a brilliant idea and head for the biggest puddle they can find. The rest of us head for shelter. There's a clump of trees next to the entrance to the playground, so we huddle beneath their branches, waiting for the bell to ring so that we can go back inside again. As if this wasn't bad enough, Craig is kicking Shane's feet, trying to make him fall over on top of me.

Shane keeps stumbling and crashing into me, accidentally-on-purpose. I try to ignore him, looking out across the playground to where Daisy and her friend Dugger are waving at me. Miss Chin is standing behind them,

with a face as black as a thunderstorm. I shiver. There's something I don't like about her, but I still can't work out what it is. As if she can hear my thoughts, her head comes up and she stares straight at me.

Craig and Shane are still trying to knock each other off balance. Yoshito looks utterly terrified and is edging as far away from them as possible. Jamie and Annabel are standing off to one side, wearing identical sailing jackets with their hoods buttoned up to their noses and ignoring everyone. I can see their eyes rolling every time Shane crashes into me, though. I bet they're secretly relieved that he's not doing it to them.

'Stop it,' I mutter under my breath.

'Eh?' Shane grunts, grabbing my arm for support, trying to regain his balance. This isn't easy: rain has turned the ground to mud, and every time we move, our feet slide around all over the place. Shane shoves his face close to mine. I can feel his hot breath on my face. Thank heavens he's not Annabel.

'I said, please stop doing that.' I'm trying to sound menacing and sort of tough when I say this, but it doesn't work. My voice comes out all wobbly because not only am I a bit scared of him, but I've also realized that I'm very close to bursting into tears.

'Right. That's IT,' Shane says, letting go of my arm and turning round to face his tormentor. 'Quit kicking me, Craig, eh? Else I'll tell Mrs McDonald.'

'Mrs McDonald can't hear you,' Craig says. 'It's only that ugly old witch looking after us, and she won't care what we do.'

Miss Chin heard him perfectly, but for once

she isn't going to react. Not this time. Normally she would turn Craig into a little heap of smoking carbon, but right here and now there are far more important things at stake. The other Blue Moon girl, the one who is also Witch Baby's pesky big sister, is staring right at her – straight *through* her, in fact.

She can see me, the Nose thinks in panic. She had to do something – *anything* – to stop this Blue Moon girl pointing an accusing finger at her and yelling 'WITCH!' at the top of her lungs. *Do something*, the Nose commands herself. But what?

The Cloak of Invisibility spell? No. It shrank in the wash.

The Memory Eraser spell? No. She's forgotten it.

Freezing rain runs down the back of the Nose's neck and an evil little smile flits across her mouth. Yessss. That's it. No need for anything too complicated. She lifts her arms up to shoulder height, her cupped hands like two claws pointing up towards the rain-soaked sky.

Easy-peasy, she thinks. Easy-peasy, cloud squeezy. Bring it on. More rain. Much more rain. So much rain that the Blue Moon girl won't be able to see anything and everyone will have to go inside.

Everyone except the Nose, who has had enough of children to last a lifetime. Her hands clench: one, two, three. Her fingers feel as if they're fizzing with electricity, all the magical power of the spell piling up as if behind a dam.

It's a big one, a huge one, she thinks, wondering if it's so strong that it will drown the children. That would be a bit of a shame. Her fingers begin to quiver uncontrollably, and the Nose decides she has to let the spell out or else her fingernails might blow off. Under her breath she whispers, '**EASY-PEASY, CLOUDSQUEEZY,**' and obediently the heavens open.

For half a second torrential rain thunders down

on the north-west of Scotland, flattening grass, drumming on roofs, dancing in puddles and soaking everything and everyone within range. But it's only half a second's worth of magical rain and then, to the Nose's alarm, everything goes horribly wrong.

Witch Baby stops whatever she was doing and spins round to face the Nose. Her big black dog vanishes in a blink, and through the rain the Nose sees that the little girl is glowing. Immediately the rain stops; except it doesn't so much stop as halt in mid-air, as if time itself has been suspended. The Nose has absolutely no idea what has gone wrong with her spell, but she's begining to suspect that Witch Baby has something to do with it.

Witch Baby heaves a huge sigh and her mouth turns down at the corners. 'No, no, no,' she says, shaking her head. 'Mumma no likeit, rain.'

Fascinating, thinks the Nose. *And I should care what your mother likes?* She considers sending a little lightning bolt whizzing across the playground to give Witch Baby a fright. Nothing too painful, just a little frizzle to remind the uppitty little wretch who's boss—

'Not wetch. Not upty. Mumma no likeit, rain. Daisy no likeit, frizzle.'

The Nose has exactly enough time to realize that Witch Baby has just read her mind when the little girl stamps her feet:

**ONE
TWO
THREE!**

claps her hands and declares, '**Snow, snow, snow.**'

The Nose shivers

232

uncontrollably. This is partly because a blizzard's worth of snowflakes is now blowing across the playground, but also because she is just beginning to realize how powerful Witch Baby is. Baby witches shouldn't be able to do this kind of advanced magic, she thinks. It's deeply impressive, but also a bit scary. Normally, at that age, spells should be weak. The Nose reminds herself how powerful her own **EASY-PEASY CLOUD SQUEEZY SPELL** had been. And now it's gone, blown away on a Witch Baby blizzard!

The Nose has to check. Witch Baby's snow spell might still be nothing more than a fluke; a magical 'blip'. Surely this will turn out to be the case. Forcing herself to relax, the Nose takes a deep breath and brings her claw-like hands up once more into the spell-casting position. There. She clenches her hands: one, two—

But she can't do it. Something is tickling

her. She drops her hands, takes another deep breath and tries again, this time counting in Latin to make the spell even stronger. *Ha, that'll teach the little madam*, she thinks.

UNUS, DUO, TRES—

She still can't do it. The same something is tickling her ribs, sending feathery twiddles into her armpits, making her want to sneeze,

brushing the extra-ticklish back of her neck with the lightest of touches – oooh, no, not there – she hates being tickled – urrrgh, stop it—

'You toppit,' a little voice informs her, and there is Witch Baby staring at her through swirling snowflakes.

'Whaaa—?' the Nose squeaks, discovering to her horror that she now cannot move so much as an eyelid. With this final spell, the upstart Witch Baby is proving that she is already a deeply, scarily and massively powerful witch. Not only can she now do more than one spell at a time, but her spells are invincible.

The Nose is beside herself with envy. Snow falls on her lashes, on her nose, on her mouth, all over her face, and she cannot do a thing to stop it.

'You toppit,' the little girl repeats, a huge smile breaking across her face. Then she turns, and is gone.

Seconds later, the Nose discovers that she is able to move again. Completely unnerved, she does the most sensible thing under the circumstances. She picks up her skirts and

flees, largely unobserved by a playground full of delighted children, all but two of whom can scarcely believe the good fortune that has brought them snow in September.

Eighteen:

A spell of good weather

I don't care what Mum says, I've never seen snow in September before. Never. Two reasons which prove this has to be Daisy's doing are: WayWoof's gone; and every so often a snowflake lands on my mouth and it tastes of strawberries. I'm hoping nobody else has noticed this, because whoever heard of strawberry-flavoured snow?

Apart from that, this is by far the best snow anyone has ever seen. Not only is it exactly the right kind of sticky snow to make perfect snowmen, it's at the ideal temperature to make sure it doesn't melt and drip over everything. The playground is filling up with an assortment of snow people: snowmen, women, cats, dogs and dinosaurs. Snow lies in drifts on the muddy slope under the trees, so we take turns sledging

on a plastic teatray that Mrs McDonald let us borrow from the staffroom. I had no idea that teatrays were so fast. We sledge in pairs, because the weight of two people makes us even faster than if there was only one on the tray. Yoshito and I shriek downhill into the playground, narrowly missing killing several innocent snowmen, and whizz across the snow, scattering nursery children before us.

I feel bad for Vivaldi, though. She would have loved this. I bet she's a really fearless sledger. It must be really horrible being stuck at home, looking out at the snow and wondering what all your friends are doing. I must remember to phone her tonight to find out if she's better yet. Craig and Shane yell to me to come and help them. They're trying to build an igloo out of bricks made by patting snow into old ice-cream tubs. They need hundreds of bricks for their igloo, so they need lots of help.

We all pitch in, thumping snow into the ice-cream tubs, turning out the snow bricks and carefully putting them in position on the igloo walls. My hands are freezing, but I don't care. This is the best day I can remember for ... oh, for ever. I check to see that Daisy is having a good time too. After all, this snow is entirely thanks to her. I scan the playground and spot her over by the trees. Yoshito is demonstrating to her and Dugger how to make angel fish in the snow. All three of them are lying on their backs in smooth patches of snow and solemnly waving one arm up and down for the angel fish's back fin, and scissoring both legs to make the tail. Like snow angels, but fishy. Perfect. Meanwhile, back to the igloo . . .

After we've made a million snow bricks, Jamie decides that it's time to organize the world's biggest ever snowball fight. Actually, it's Jamie who organizes us into two armies and tells us the rules. He turns out to be very bossy, but we're all having such fun that we let him go ahead and be a dictator. I'm in his army, Jamie says, because I'm quite strong for a girl. Annabel isn't in his army, because he says she's a complete pain, smells like a dead haddock, and besides, she's his sister.

First, he says we have to gather ammunition and stockpile it. This means I have to make tons of snowballs while he stands around blowing on his hands and sorting them into little piles. Then he explains that we need to find ourselves an easily defended stronghold. Poor Jamie — he's only eleven and already he sounds like he's been in the army for ever. He's carrying about

twenty of my carefully stockpiled snowballs in
his jacket over to his easily defended stronghold
when Annabel launches the first attack.

For someone who smells like a dead haddock, her aim is impressive. A snowball arcs through the air and smacks off the back of Jamie's unprotected neck.

'AAAAAAAAAH! You big CHEATER!' he roars, and we're off. It's WAR. The air fills with snowballs as well as snowflakes. Nobody is spared. There are thuds followed by shrieks as snowballs find their targets, and wails as small people are mown down in the rush to gather more ammunition. There are grunts as snowballs slam into people's backs, screams of revenge and the occasional ghastly silence as we all hold our breath and pray that the staffroom window hasn't smashed after a direct hit from a hard-packed snowball.

I'm shivering, my hands are two useless throbbing lumps, my fingers like frozen sausages, and I've fallen over so often that my legs are caked with slush. I don't think I've ever felt so good in my whole life. This is the most brilliant day ever. Snow is still falling steadily as Mrs McDonald comes out into the playground and calls us all over. Although it

isn't even lunch time yet, she is debating whether to send us all home early because of the snow.

'NOOOOOOO,' wails Shane. 'I don't want to go home. Ochhh, come on, Mrs McDonald. I haven't even finished building my snow dinosaur yet.'

I don't want to go home either. It's too much fun being here, playing with everyone. We're all having such a good time. I look around the playground. Everyone's staring at Mrs McDonald with big spaniel-eyes, willing her not to send us home.

'Pleeeease?' Craig begs. 'Let us stay on? We could even write about snow for our weather project. But that would mean we'd have to stay and do some more . . . er . . . research.'

Brilliant! What a good idea. Jamie gives Craig the thumbs-up and Shane slaps him on the shoulder in a friendly way. I stare at Mrs McDonald and I can sense her weakening. We all smile harder and cross our fingers tightly. Oh, please . . .

Mrs McDonald sighs. She knows when she's beaten. 'Very well,' she says. 'You can all stay until the little ones go home at lunch time, but no longer than that. And I must warn you: if it keeps snowing, I'll have to send you home right away. Any more snow and the roads will be blocked and then your mums and dads won't be able to get here to pick you up.'

Miraculously, the words have barely left her mouth when the snow stops, as if someone has turned it off with a switch. Fortunately I'm the only one who knows that somebody has, though not with a switch, but a spell.

Woo-hoo, Witch Baby. Respect.

*

The Chin skids and slithers in the snow, her leaky boots hardly able to grip the pavement's icy surface. Unable to run without falling over, she has slowed down to a fast walk, but this does nothing to stop her panicking. Her mind is full of terrible thoughts of blaring sirens, policemen and jail cells; she's sure she'll stagger back to

Arkon House in time to see the poor Toad being led away in chains. She promises that if she does make it home without being arrested, she'll try to undo the spells that so cruelly transformed Miss McPhee and the postman. Trying to remember how to reverse them, the Chin is so wrapped up in her thoughts that she steps straight out in front of a car.

There's an outraged **BEEEEEPAOOOGAAAA** from its horn, a shriek of brakes, and then something grabs her from behind and hurls her safely across the road and onto the icy pavement on the other side.

'Ahhh, Miss Chin, we meet again,' a familiar voice gasps in her ear. 'So very fortunate that I was passing, yes?'

Fortunate, thinks the Chin, face down in the slush. *Not the first word that springs to mind.* The weight pinning her to the pavement

shifts, and there, kneeling by her side, is Mr Haruskashi, his face full of kindly concern.

'Don't move, dear lady. I shall summon an ambulance to take you to the hospital, and the police will be on their way in due course—'

The word 'police' acts on the Chin like an electric shock. Batting Mr Harukashi aside, she leaps to her feet . . . totters . . . and, with a squeak of dismay, discovers that she's ripped the sole off one of her boots. Stifling an oath, she hops about in the snow, trying to remove the useless item of footwear. Despite her miraculous recovery, Mr Harukashi still insists on offering help.

'No. NO. NO,' the Chin mutters. 'I'm fine. There's no need for all this fuss. No, really, there's no call for an ambulance. Don't be silly. Just as soon as I get rid of this useless, stupid, boot—' She loses her balance and falls on top of Mr Harukashi, nearly bringing them both crashing down to the ground. Mr Harukashi teeters, staggers, grabs onto a lamppost for support and manages to remain upright despite the Chin's added weight. Propping her against the lamppost while she struggles with her boot, he tries to reason with her.

'Dear lady, at least allow me to drive you home, yes? You cannot possibly walk home barefoot through deep snow.'

He has a point there. The Chin looks down at her feet: one is clad in leaky leather; the other bare, white and, she realizes with a howl of terror, in full possession of seven toes.*

OOOOOps.

Time to go home before anyone notices.

---

* These are a permanent side-effect of one of the Chin's earliest spells. She'd been playing 'This little piggy' with her sisters and couldn't resist showing off.

Mr Harukashi is too busy gazing into the Chin's eyes to notice her extra toes, and besides, he has a very comfortable car. In truth, the Chin is cold, wet and feeling rather sorry for herself. A lift home would be very welcome, and if Arkon House is surrounded by police, she will let Mr Harukashi get out of his car first, and then she will steal it to make a getaway. With a girly little sigh, the Chin tucks her arm into that of Mr Harukashi, and together they pick their way through the snow to his waiting car.

'But aren't you pleased?' the Toad asks, passing a steaming cup of hot nettle soup across to her sneezing sister.

The Nose, no longer magically disguised as Miss Chin, is immersed up to her own vast

nostrils in a hot bath. She's trying to thaw herself out after taking a short cut home from school that plunged her up to her eyebrows in a snowdrift.

'Pleas-aaa-aahhh-ker-CHOOo-pleased?' she gasps. 'Pleased about wha-aaah-ahhh-choo-what?'

The Toad rolls her big yellow eyes. 'Pleased that our dear little Witch Baby isn't becoming too human,' she continues. 'Pleased that you don't have to go to school any more. Pleased that our dear baby appears to be a very wicked witch indeed.'

At this, the Nose snorts, causing two huge ripples to run across the surface of the bathwater. 'PFFFffffFF. It was only a little snow spell,' she hisses, secretly furious that a witch as old and as experienced as her could possibly have been out-spelled by a mere Witch Baby.

'A little snow spell?' the Toad croaks, aghast. 'How can you say that? Our house is practically buried in snow. You fell into a snowdrift that was taller than you are. It was an enormous snow spell. If one of us had cast it, we'd still be celebrating.'

'**Harrrrumph**,' says the Nose, but she knows the Toad is right. Witch Baby is shaping up to be a very, very wicked witch indeed. However, far from being delighted that she is doing so well, the Nose is feeling very worried. What if the little girl becomes so big and powerful that she ends up stronger that the three Sisters of Hiss put together? When it's time to take her away from her human family and teach her how to become a Proper Hiss, what if she doesn't want to leave?

What then?

Downstairs, the front door slams. The Chin is home. The sound of Mr Harukashi's car driving away fades into silence. Upstairs, the Nose pulls out the plug and gets up to find a towel. The Toad hops down to greet the

Chin, wondering if her trip to the library was a success. She finds her sister sitting at the dining table, riffling through a huge book of spells. On the Chin's lap is the postman-cat and, on the table, dropping poo all over the place, is Miss McPhee, still a sparrow, but hopefully, if all goes well, not a sparrow for much longer. Mercifully, the Chin made it home without

being arrested, so she is about to keep her promise to restore the cat and the sparrow to human form.

The Toad frowns. It doesn't look as if the Chin has had a successful day. She doesn't seem to have made any money whatsoever. There's a distinct lack of sacks marked **SWAG**, suitcases of banknotes or even little velvet drawstring bags of uncut diamonds. The Toad's frown deepens. It's beginning to look like they'll be dining on rats and nettles for a long time yet. *Honestly,* the Toad thinks, *if I'd been the one sent out to make money, we'd be up to our eyeballs in gold by now.* But she knows better than to breathe so much as a word of complaint against her Sisters. When you're as small as the Toad, you learn to keep your thoughts to yourself and secretly cook up a spell to multiply the contents of the Sisters of Hiss's bank account one thousand

times. One thousand times their last fourteen
pounds and twenty-two pence ought to be
enough to buy a pizza or two. Her warty lips
hardly moving as she multiplies inside her head,
the Toad meekly hops into the kitchen and gets
on with it.

Nineteen:

Finally, spotless

By lunch time, the playground is transformed. We all helped Craig and Shane to build their igloo – even Mrs McDonald and Mr Fox, the janitor. With every single one of us making snow bricks in ice-cream tubs, we were able to make an amazing igloo. It's enormous; big enough for us all to sit inside comfortably. When Craig carefully put the last brick in place in the roof, we all cheered. Mrs McDonald took loads of photographs because she said nobody would believe that we'd had snow in September. Then we all crawled inside and imagined what it must be like to live in an igloo instead of a house.

'Freezing,' moaned Shane. 'And there's nowhere to plug in your TV.'

'Daddy says our house is as cold as an igloo,' Annabel admitted, adding, 'He's wrong.

Our house is much colder. In the winter, our toothbrushes freeze.' *

'Well, I really like it in here,' said Craig. 'I'm not going home. I want to live here for ever.'

'Don't be daft,' said Shane. 'It'll all be melted by tomorrow.'

At this, we all fell silent. The igloo had taken us all so long to make that we hadn't had any time to really play in it yet. Nobody wanted it to melt.

'It's always horrible when snowmen melt,' Jamie said, blowing into his cupped hands to warm them up. 'When all that's left of them the next day is a couple of bits of coal and a carrot . . .'

'And a scarf,' said Yoshito.

* Nope. With breath as bad as Annabel's, I can't believe she ever uses any kind of toothbrush, frozen or not.

'And their smile,' I said.

'Whatever are you talking about?' demanded Annabel. 'How can a snowman leave its smile behind?'

I was about to explain that in our family, when we make a snowman, we always give it a smile made out of little pebbles, but Yoshito got in first.

'Snowmen leave their smiles with us when they melt,' she said. 'I can see the smile on all our faces. We've all got one. Look at us. We are all smiling.'

And she's right. Here we are, sitting inside the igloo that we built because we all worked together. We haven't had any fights, we've looked after the little ones, we've had a great day, and now, at the end of it, we're all smiling from ear to ear. The only thing missing is Vivaldi. All of a sudden I feel bad for having such a good time when she's been stuck inside. Poor Vivaldi.

I look at Daisy and an idea begins to form inside my mind. I have no idea how strong Daisy's spells are, but I think I'm about to find out. I crawl across the snow to where she's sitting and squat down beside her.

'Daze . . .' I whisper in her ear.

'**Tickly no, no, toppit, Lillil,**' she squeaks, pushing me away.

'Sorry, Daisy. Erm, you know how Vivaldi isn't at school today?'

Daisy is silent, poking her index finger into the snow between her knees. **Poke**, **poke**, **poke**, she goes, making little dots in the snow. I carry on.

'Poor Vivaldi is stuck at home with spots. Poor her. She can't come out to play with us because of those horrible spots.'

Daisy looks up at me, and for one second I catch a glimpse of something dazzlingly bright in her eyes. Then she sighs and pokes at the snow again. 'What you want, Lillil?'

Well. I can take a hint. *Do get to the point, Lily.*

'I need you to make Vivaldi's spots go away, Daisy. Could you do that? Please?'

Daisy ignores me, but a little shiver goes down my spine when I see what she's busy

doing. The snow between her feet is pitted with dots where she's been poking it with her fingers, but now she's humming to herself as she smoothes it out with the palm of her hand. And once it's perfectly smooth, I see that she's drawn a circle on the outside. A circle that looks a bit like a face.

'Thank you, Daisy,' I whisper. **Woo-hooo**. **That Witch Baby**. *Don't mess with her.*

Outside, the bell starts to ring and it's time to go home. For the very first time since I came to this school, I really, really don't want to go.

'See you tomorrow, pal.' Craig whacks me

on the shoulder in a friendly way and runs off across the playground.

'The snowman gave you the best smile,' Yoshito says, waving goodbye.

We walk across the playground shivering because it was actually warm inside our igloo. Shane is walking beside me.

'That was just the coolest fun ever, eh, Lily?' he says, turning back to look at the igloo. He gives the air a couple of punches like a footballer who's scored a goal. 'Aw, that was just magic.'

He's right. It was. Magic, in every way.

Back home, there's a set of smallish footprints leading across the snow from our gate to the front doorstep and back. When Mum opens the door, there's a note lying on the doormat. Before I can pick it up, Daisy grabs it and runs away, cackling to herself.

'Come on, sweetheart,' Mum sighs. 'You can't read yet, silly.'

Daisy gives Mum the Stare of Doom and peers at the note in her hand. 'Not silly. Daisy reddit now.'

I make a grab for the note but Daisy's too quick. She runs into the kitchen and hides under the table. When she does stuff like this, I want to scream. She may have done the most amazing snow spell in the whole wide world, but right now she's just my very, very annoying pesky little sister.

'Oh, come on then,' I groan. 'You win, Daze. You read it to us. What does it say?'

Daisy beams and looks up at me. 'Daisy says spots all gone 'way—' But whatever she was about to say next is lost for all time because she's just caught sight of what Mum's been baking today.

WOW. What an incredible cake. It's enormous, covered in snowy white icing and decorated with leaves made of dark chocolate. It's absolutely beautiful. Mum looks slightly embarrassed.

'I got a bit carried away,' she says. 'I mean, it's not as if it's anyone's birthday or anything . . .'

Daisy's eyes are wide with wonder. '**Oooooh**,' she breathes, gazing at the cake in awe. '**Ooooh**, Mumma. Wantit. Wantit now, bigbit.'

'It's an un-birthday cake,' I decide, picking up the note which Daisy has completely forgotten about since catching sight of The Cake. I unfold it:

> *Dear Lil* (it says),
> *My spots suddenly fell off* and Mum says I'm better now so please come for supper tonight. Can't wait 2CU.*
> *Lots of love,*
> *your friend,*
> *Vivaldi*

I'm not kidding!
P.S. Mum's making pizza.
P.P.S. I know the most amazing hill
for sledging.

I look up. Vivaldi's spots fell off? I want to hug Daisy and tell the whole world what a wee star she is, but she has her face buried in a colossal slab of Mum's un-birthday cake. Even I know better than to disturb her right now. Her eyes are closed in utter bliss. I know just how she feels. Today has been the best of fun, there's cake and soon I'm going to my best friend's house for tea. I feel so happy, I think I might be in danger of exploding.

So I do the next best thing. Down go my hands, up go my feet and I turn three cartwheels down the hall. Taaa-daaa!

'Lily, for heaven's sake,' Mum groans.

'Blue,' mutters Daisy, but I can tell she's not

really paying attention because today my pants
are pink.

Later that afternoon, Vivaldi and I are walking
back to her house for supper, taking it in turns
to drag the sledge behind us.

'. . . and then my spots fell off and dropped
onto the page I was reading . . .' Vivaldi

groans. 'It was disgusting. I had to flush them down the loo. **Eeeeurrrch**. Right, it's your turn.'

I take the rope out of her hand and follow her up the hill. It's very steep, and brilliant for sledging, but not so brilliant for hauling the sledge back up again.

'Isn't this just the most amazing snow, though?' I gasp, stopping to catch my breath and look out over the white fields. 'You have to admit, Daisy is pretty impressive.'

'How come her snow spell is still working?' Vivaldi asks, her breath making icy clouds in front of her mouth.

'I have no idea.' I'd been wondering the same thing. It's been her longest spell yet. 'But,' I add, 'I'm positive she's becoming more powerful – she kept the snow spell going *and* made your spots fall off. That's two spells at once.

It's hardly surprising that
WayWoof's been gone
all day.'

'I love WayWoof,'
says Vivaldi. 'I wish
I had a dog like
her. If she ever
has puppies,
can I have
one?'

'Promise,' I say, imagining a litter of tiny, stinky, occasionally invisible puppies. Wow. How weird would that be? But right now I'd give anything to have WayWoof with us. It's getting dark, and although I'm not in the least bit scared, there's something deeply comforting about the company of a dog, even an invisible one.

We walk past the amazing round house where Yoshito lives with her dad. The twilight sky is reflected in their fish-shaped pool and it looks like something out of a film or a magazine, but I don't think I'd like to live there much. I prefer our scruffy garden with its hiding places and trees to climb. We walk on, past Mishnish Castle, where bossy Jamie and smelly Annabel live. At least, I think that's where they live, but I can't see a castle or even a house up there; only a long road which winds past lawns and disappears into trees. It must be an amazing house, though, because Annabel's always going on and on about it.

Then, without saying anything, Vivaldi and I both start walking very fast. It seems

to have got a lot darker, although the setting sun is still blazing through the trees. We're almost at the gates of Arkon House now and I can see that Vivaldi is as nervous as I am. This is because Arkon House is rumoured to be haunted. It certainly looks as if it might be. It's got ruined turrets, loads of dark, dark windows, a massive front door and a really creepy swimming pool full of rotting leaves. If I had to describe it in one word, the word would be 'Yyyyyyeeeeargggghhhhh'.

Vivaldi grabs my arm. 'Look,' she whispers. 'The front door's opening . . .'

She's right. It is. Suddenly I know that I don't want to hear the eeeecreeeak of the door's hinges or see who or what is about to come out from behind it.

At least, not now. I look at Vivaldi. I can see that she's just like me: half curious to find out if Arkon House really is haunted, and half terrified in case it is. Then, in the deepening silence, my tummy gives a loud rumble and the front door of Arkon House slams shut. Time for supper.

'Race you back home,' Vivaldi says, and we flee through the woods towards the setting sun.

Twenty:

Another story

'It hasn't worked,' complains the Nose, glaring at the sparrow and the cat, who are stubbornly refusing to be changed back into their human forms.

'**Miayowly, yowl**,' agrees the cat.

The sparrow rolls her beady eyes and ejects a pellet of bird poo. This is her way of showing just how fed up she is with the Hisses.

'It has worked,' mutters the Chin. 'It just happens to be a slow spell. It takes a long time to undo what was done in haste. The spell has to start from the inside and work its way out. First of all it has to wipe their memories . . .'

'**Mao**? **Yee**? **Howl**?' the postman bleats, utterly confused as the spell begins to take effect. What is he? he wonders. A bird? A man?

An envelope?

'Baa, squeak, WOOf,' adds the sparrow, falling over sideways.

'. . . and then,' continues the Chin, 'we'll have to put them back where we found them. I've worked it all out. We've got just enough time if we get a move on. They won't return to their human form until dawn and—'

'Hang on,' interrupts the Toad. 'We can't dump the cat – sorry, the postman, where we found him. That would mean leaving him on our own doorstep. And that would be a very bad idea, wouldn't it?'

'Why don't we just deposit him back at his post office then?' suggests the Nose, adding, 'And we can drop the teacher-sparrow off in the staffroom at the school.'

'Brilliant!' says the Chin. 'That way, when they wake up, they'll both assume they've fallen asleep at work.'

'But . . . nobody else will think that,' the Toad mutters.

'Who cares what anybody else thinks?' snaps the Nose. 'The point is to get rid of them without being found out. This way nobody will connect their reappearance with us, and as long as they don't remember what happened to them, everything will be all right. And,' she adds happily, 'I'll never, ever have to be a teacher again, and nor will you, Chin dear.'

'I'll get the broomsticks,' says the Toad, delighted at the prospect of a night-flight. 'Oooh, it's been ages since we did anything like this . . .' She heads for the broom cupboard while the Chin pounces

on the sparrow and the Nose grabs the cat.

Fur and feathers fly everywhere. The cat and the sparrow don't understand why they have to be tied up, but the Nose and the Chin understand all too well. If, by some awful twist of fate, they didn't make it to the post office and the school by the dawn deadline, the cat and the sparrow would still return to their human forms. In mid-flight. The idea of trying to steer a broomstick with a struggling human on board is enough to throw all three Hisses into a panic.

Several metres of string, many muttered oaths and a few carrier bags later, they're ready to go. The Nose has a nasty scratch across her left hand and the Chin is speckled with sparrow poo, but the cat and the sparrow are trussed up with string and wrapped in carrier bags with only their heads poking out. The Toad opens the front door and the three sisters head out into the sunset with their unwilling passengers firmly tied to their broomsticks.

'What d'you say we pick up a takeaway pizza on the way home?' suggests the Toad, hopping onto the Chin's broomstick.

'We'll see,' says the Nose, pulling on her wraparound flying goggles. She's unable to resist checking her elegant reflection in her broomstick's rear-view mirror.

There's a **CRACK**, and the mirror shatters into a thousand pieces.

'Great,' mutters the Chin. 'More expense . . .'

Behind them, the door to Arkon House slams shut. Silently the two broomsticks rise into the night sky, heading south.

I'm up in Daisy's bedroom, reading her a bed-time story. At times like this I completely forget that my little sister is really a Witch Baby. Tonight she's wearing her pink rabbit pyjamas and she smells of baby powder. She looks so sweet I could almost eat her. I inch closer, hoping that she'll snuggle against me like she sometimes does if she's in the right mood. Sadly, tonight Daisy has other ideas. She bats me away and struggles to sit up.

'Want nother story,' she says, looking sideways at her shadow on the wall beside her bed.

'Come on, Daze,' I groan. 'I've already read five. Heaven's sake, surely that's enough?'

'Not nuff. Want notha one.'

To hear is to obey. Otherwise . . . well, who knows what she might do?

'Notta book. Wanta mouff story.'

A mouth story? Oh, help. Those are tricky. A mouth story means she wants me to make one up. I stare at the wall, trying to think of something.

'Once upon a time,' I begin, 'there was a dog who was invisible . . .'

'Not vinzible,' Daisy mutters.

'Whatever,' I snap. I hate being interrupted before I've even started. Heaving a huge sigh, I carry on, 'The dog had eyes like dinner plates, a tail like a loo-brush and a black, black coat that had never been brushed . . .'

'**Ahhh**,' Daisy sighs, popping her thumb into her mouth and snuggling down. Obviously she thinks I'm going to tell her a long story and all she has to do is lie there and enjoy it. She's wrong. I'm tired too. All that igloo-building was exhausting. I don't want to spend the entire night sitting on the floor, making up stories for *Queen Daisy*. No way. I'm not doing all the work. I decide that Daisy has to help me with her story, so I prompt her: 'And who do you think this dog belonged to . . . ?'

Daisy fixes me with a withering stare. I stare back. Finally, when she realizes that there will be no more story until she comes up with something, she drags her thumb out of her mouth, peers at it, sighs heavily and says, '**Pinsess Dackula**.'

There. See what I mean? One minute Daisy is a fluffy little tot and the next she's unmasked as the founder member of the Association of Ladies with Pointy Hats and Cauldrons. **Woo-hOo**. I'd better behave.

'Ahem. Yes. Princess Dracula's dog was very happy doing doggy things like sniffing, snuffling, licking—'

'Bottoms,' Daisy adds, but I think I'll simply ignore that.

'— and playing chase-its-own-tail. But the thing the dog loved best of all was the little girl.' I sneak a look at Daisy. She's staring at the ceiling with a wistful expression on her face. 'The little girl was very happy too.

Tormenting her big sister, casting snow spells and generally causing havoc. But best of all, the little girl loved the dog—'

'WAYWOOF!' Daisy wailed, loud enough to make me jump. 'Wantit WayWoof. Love WayWoof.' And to my dismay, she burst into tears.

Oh dear. This is not going well. Poor Daisy. I haul her out of bed and sit her on my lap, but

I can't cheer her up. She's crying her heart out now and the front of her bunny pyjamas is all soggy and cold.

'WaaaaayyyyWooOoo, WooOoo,' she howls, big tears spilling out of her eyes and down her little face. Any minute now, Mum's going to come up to find out what on earth is going on. I rock Daisy from side to side and make shushing sounds, but it doesn't make any difference.

Outside, it has begun to rain hard, so I guess that will be the end of Daisy's snow spell. Which means . . .

'WayyyWoOo,' she snuffles, wriggling off my lap to grab at an invisible something that I can't see yet. There's a patch of shadow forming between her outstretched arms and the faint beginnings of a dreadful smell. The snow spell is officially over and rain is pouring down outside, reminding me of our poor igloo standing in the middle of the dark school playground. Soon it will start dissolving into slush. There's a sympathetic sigh close to my ear, followed by a familiar panting sound and there, with Daisy's arms wrapped round her neck, is our very own WayWoof.

Hoorah! I'm so pleased to see her that I wrap my arms around her black, black unbrushed coat and hug her. Tight.

'More. More story, Lillil,' my baby sister demands, clambering back into bed. With a bound, WayWoof follows, her expression vaguely apologetic. Normally, Daisy and I would never let her climb all

over our beds, but tonight isn't normal. We settle down, all three of us.

WayWoof releases a pungent cloud of dog-gas and falls fast asleep.

I'm nearly asleep too. It's warm and cosy in Daisy's room, and outside I can hear the rain falling, flowing along gutters, down drains and eventually out into the sea, where it will join up with all the melted bits of Daisy's snow spell. It's a lovely sound, rain. It makes me so sleepy.

I look at WayWoof. She's twitchily dreaming. She looks really sweet. Vivaldi's right: puppies would be amazing . . .

Beside me, Daisy wriggles round and sits up. 'More,' she mutters, staring at me, but not really at me. In fact it's as if she's staring right through me.

'More WayWoofs,' she decides, her mouth curving up into a dreamy smile. 'Lots more WayWoofs,' she adds, then she flings herself

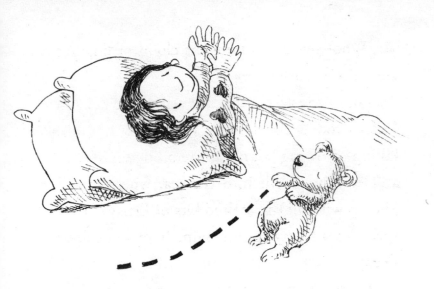

backwards onto her pillow, claps her hands and her teddy floats up off the floor and into her arms. Her eyelashes flutter, and within seconds she's fast asleep.

More WayWoofs? What has Daisy done?

Without waking her, I turn over to stare at the sleeping WayWoof. She doesn't look any different, but then she wouldn't, would she? Not at first, anyway. Mind you, everything I

know about dogs and puppies could be written on the back of a postage stamp. I need to ask Vivaldi. She knows all about dogs. I'll phone her tomorrow when I get back from sch—

Then I remember. Vivaldi will be at school tomorrow. I won't have to phone her because I'll see her first thing in the morning. HOORAH! I can hardly wait. With her there, everything will be all right. And, I think, just before I fall asleep: *Tomorrow is Thursday – so that means Sticky Toffee Pudding.*

School? I can't wait.

Dawn is just breaking outside the staffroom window as Miss McPhee stirs in her sleep and stretches out her wings to air her feathers.

There's a **crash** as the electric kettle topples off the top of the fridge and spills its contents all over a pile of maths jotters. There will be great happiness when the children learn of their jotters' fate. For now, though, all is confusion as Miss McPhee jolts awake.

'AAARGH!' she yells. 'Whaaa—?' Then, recognizing her surroundings, she squawks, 'What on earth . . . ?'

Whatever is she doing, sleeping in the staffroom? And the dreams she's just had . . . Miss McPhee shivers. She must be coming down with something, she decides. Falling asleep at work? Why did nobody wake her? She must have been asleep for hours. Time to go home,

she thinks, before anyone finds her snoozing at school. Buttoning her coat up to her chin, she lets herself out of the school by a side door and begins to walk back to her house, just like she did the day she vanished.

Soon she will discover that she's been missing for some time – the police will ask her loads of questions that she won't be able to answer. But for now she's going back home to her own bed, where she's going to burrow under the duvet and catch a few hours' sleep before it's time to get up for work.

Across the road, the postman wraps his paws round an enormous mouse and sinks his teeth into its neck.

There's a muffled **yOwl**, a scream, and the postman wakes up to discover he's trying to eat a mailbag.

'EH? What the—?' he gasps, his eyes

barely able to focus on the familiar
interior of the sorting office. Scratching
his head, he slowly climbs to his feet and stares
at the clock on the wall. Five thirty, it reads.
Thank heavens the morning shift doesn't start
for another half-hour – otherwise the other
postmen would have had something to say
about him sleeping on the job. Yawning widely,
he shakes his head and stares at the clock again.
He can hardly believe his eyes. He must have

fallen asleep last night, but he can't remember anything about it. His brain feels as if it's full of soft, grey fog. He decides that the best thing to do is go home, grab a shower and try to get some sleep. Obviously he's been overdoing it. Too many late nights, too many early mornings and far too much work. Definitely time to book that holiday he's been promising himself. But not anywhere with cats. The postman shudders. He's never liked cats – or dogs for that matter. But now, for some reason, just the thought of cats makes him feel very odd indeed.

Whistling loudly to cheer himself up, the postman lets himself out of the back door of the post office and heads for home. He's ravenous. He can't wait to sink his teeth into something tastier than his mailbag. Whatever was he dreaming about?

Dawn is breaking over the roof of Arkon House as the Sisters of Hiss bring their broomsticks down on the edge of their empty swimming pool. They're feeling very pleased with themselves. Mission accomplished. The cat and the sparrow have been returned safely with their

memories of their time at Arkon House wiped clean. Not only that, but as the Toad points out, 'We used magic and nobody noticed.'

'So what?' says the Nose, rolling her eyes as if to say, *Big deal*.

'So what?' the Toad insists. 'Nobody noticed, is what. That means we can start to use magic again if we're very careful. Doesn't it?'

The Nose sucks air in through her teeth and shakes her head slowly from side to side.

The Chin looks as if she's just sat on a hedgehog.

But the Toad is unstoppable. 'Come on, girls,' she says. 'Lighten up. Where's your sense of adventure? We're going to be stuck here for years while we wait for our Witch Baby to be ready. We may as well try to enjoy ourselves, yes?'

The Chin and the Nose both look as if

they're being mauled by small lions. Enjoy themselves?

The very idea!

The Toad groans, but she's determined not to give up. 'Look, as long as we're very, very, very careful not to do anything too huge or too weird, I can't see any reason why we shouldn't use a tiny speck of magic now and then just to make our lives a little bit easier.'

There's a long silence, then the Chin finally says, 'Exactly what sort of spells did you have in mind?'

The Toad clasps her webbed feet together and begins, 'Well – I thought that for starters we could clean out our pool and fill it with—'

'Champagne!' interrupts the Nose. 'Let's fill it with fizz.'

The Chin gapes at the Nose as if she cannot believe her ears, but the Nose ignores her.

'GREAT IDEA!' yells the Toad, then adds, 'Consider it done.'

There's a **whoosh**, a **sploosh** and a long

series of popping sounds as if thousands of champagne corks are being fired at once.

'NOW HANG ON!' the Chin roars. 'Stop this right now.'

The Toad slumps. *Oh, dear*, she thinks. *I just knew I wasn't going to get away with—*

'WHAT?' bawls the Nose. 'What are we waiting for? What's the matter?'

The Chin draws herself up to her full

height and folds her arms across her chest. She frowns and points her chin towards where the swimming pool is now glittering, sparkling and fizzing in the morning sunlight. She clears her throat.

'Nobody is to use that pool,' she says,

holding up her hands to stop the Nose and the Toad interrupting her. 'NOBODY,' she repeats firmly, then her face creases up in a smile and she emits a girlish cackle; 'nobody is to dip as much as a toe in that champagne until I have tried it first!' And she bounds across the lawn, then, with a shriek of delight, dives headlong into the pool.

Pausing only to magic up a stylish bikini for herself, the Nose follows her sister into the sparkling liquid.

The Toad smiles as her Sisters' shrieks
and cackles drift through the open windows
of the kitchen at Arkon House. Inside, all is

transformed. The pantry is piled high with pizzas, chocolate and tins of cherries. The breadbin is overflowing with croissants, currant buns and bagels and the freezer is full of ice cream. For the Sisters of Hiss, the good times have finally begun. Waiting for Witch Baby is going to be the best fun they've ever had.

witch baby and me

My life is in ruins. Here's why:

★ I have a baby sister called Daisy. She's not a *baby* baby, she's a *witch* baby.

★ Only *I* know this (that she's a witch baby). Everyone else thinks she's sweet and adorable.

★ Daisy's summoned up an invisible dog called WayWoof to be her pet. People can smell WayWoof but they can't see him – so they think the smell is me.

But worst of all is:

★ Mum and Dad have decided that we're moving house. To the far, far North of Scotland. Which means I'll never see my friends again!

978 0552 55676 7